Pony 🐎 Club Secrets

Flame and the
Rebel Riders

The Pony Club Secrets series:

1. Mystic and the Midnight Ride

2. Blaze and the Dark Rider

3. Destiny and the Wild Horses

4. Stardust and the Daredevil Ponies

5. Comet and the Champion's Cup

6. Storm and the Silver Bridle

7. Fortune and the Golden Trophy

8. Victory and the All-Stars Academy

9. Flame and the Rebel Riders

Also available in the series:

Issie and the Christmas Pony

(Christmas special)

Coming soon...

10. Angel and the Flying Stallions

PONY CLUB SECRETS

Flame and the Rebel Riders

STACY GREGG

HarperCollins *Children's Books*

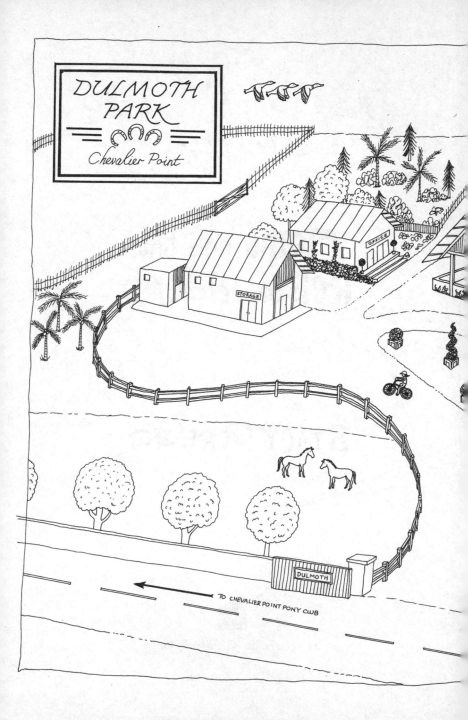

DULMOTH
PARK

Chevalier Point

OFFICE

STORAGE

DULMOTH

TO CHEVALIER POINT PONY CLUB

With thanks to my wonderful editor Lizzie Ryley

www.stacygregg.co.uk

Congratulations and thanks to Ashlea Hartland and Breanna Payne, the winners of our "Name a Pony" competition. Ashlea's horse Tokyo and Breanna's horse Sebastian both appear in this book. Also there's a name change for the International League for the Protection of Horses. The real-life organisation is now known as Horse Welfare, so we've swapped to this from now on too!

First published in Great Britain by HarperCollins *Children's Books* in 2010.
HarperCollins *Children's Books* is a division of HarperCollins*Publishers* Ltd,
77–85 Fulham Palace Road, Hammersmith, London, W6 8JB.

1

Text copyright © Stacy Gregg 2010
Illustrations © Fiona Land 2010

ISBN-13 978-0-00-729929-4

The author and illustrator assert the moral right to be identified
as the author and illustrator of the work.

Typeset in Adobe Garamond by Palimpsest Book Production Limited,
Grangemouth, Stirlingshire
Printed and bound in England by Clays Ltd, St Ives plc

Chapter 1

The envelope in the schoolbag didn't look like it could cause any trouble. It was a plain envelope, with no airs or graces about it, brown and slender with just two words written on the front in felt tip: Isadora Brown.

Issie had shoved the envelope into her schoolbag and promptly forgotten about it. It had nestled overnight beside her pencil case, getting squashed by her school jumper, and might have stayed hidden there if her mum hadn't opened the bag to get her lunchbox out.

"What's this?" Mrs Brown asked, picking the envelope up off the floor.

"My end-of-year report. You have to sign it so I can take it back to school," Issie said, glancing at the envelope as she picked up the last piece of toast on her plate and stood up from the table. "Thanks for breakfast, Mum," she called over her shoulder as she hurried out of the kitchen with the toast in hand, heading for the laundry. It was seven thirty and Issie was running late. Today was pony-club rally day and Tom Avery, Chevalier Point's head instructor, had offered to pick up the girls and their horses in his truck from the River Paddock at eight. Stella and Kate would already be there by now, grooming and bandaging their horses. And Issie was still in her pyjamas!

"Have you seen my white jodhpurs?" she shouted out to her mum from the laundry. "You know, the good ones? They're not in my room…"

Mrs Brown walked into the laundry, but didn't answer. She had opened the envelope and was holding the report in her hand. She had a stunned expression on her face. "Isadora! Have you read this?"

Issie winced. Her mother only used her full name when she was in trouble. "No…" she said. "Mr Monagatti said we're supposed to give them to our parents to open." Issie looked at the piece of paper in her mum's hand. "I didn't think it would be… is it really that bad?"

"Bad?" Mrs Brown shook her head in disbelief. "Issie, it's brilliant! This is one of the most glowing school reports I've ever read! You're topping the class in maths and science. You've got A+ for your English and history marks. Your form teacher describes you as 'above average in all subjects'."

"I'm still useless at French," Issie said, "Mr Canning says my vocab is OK, but I have trouble with my—"

"Issie," Mrs Brown said, "French aside, this is a really terrific report card. Why didn't you show it to me? You should be thrilled with it… Issie?"

Issie's head had disappeared into the laundry basket as she desperately hunted for the missing jods. "I forgot about it!" she said as she began to dig frantically through the clothes. "I went over to Kate's after school and… Ohmygod! There they are!" Issie emerged triumphant with the jodhpurs. She looked at her watch. Seven forty! "Mum, can you give me a lift down to the paddock? I'll never make it in time on my bike."

Mrs Brown wasn't listening. She was still poring over the report card. "Look at this! Your average mark for the term was 87 per cent!"

"Mum!" Issie was frantic. "Can't we talk about it later? I'm going to be late for pony club!"

"Oh, don't let me hold you up with my brief moment of parental pride," Mrs Brown said sarcastically, "I'm sure you don't want to keep the horses waiting…"

Issie's mum didn't stop talking about the report card all the way to the River Paddock. Then when they arrived, she embarrassed Issie by going on about it again in front of the other girls and even telling Avery about her results!

"My school report was hopeless!" Stella grumbled as they loaded the horses on to Avery's truck. "All my teachers went on and on about how I don't pay enough attention in class. I told my mum that I'd pay more attention if they weren't so boring!"

"I just about fell asleep in French class the other day," Kate agreed.

"I know! I can't stand French!" Stella groaned. "Mr Canning is bonkers. I can't understand a word he's saying!"

"It's like he's speaking a foreign language!" Kate added, and the three girls burst into giggles.

"Are you going to take it again for fifth form?" Issie asked.

Kate nodded. "I guess so."

"I can't believe you're talking about this!" Stella said. "I don't even want to think about what subjects I'm taking next year. Only one more week of school to go and then seven weeks off! I'm going to spend every single day riding and I vow not to speak a single word of French!"

"What about puissance?" Issie said. "That's a French word."

"Then I shall refuse to jump them!" Stella said theatrically and the three girls fell about laughing again.

Stella and Kate were Issie's best friends. Issie's mum always said the three of them were like sisters – which was funny since the girls didn't look anything alike. Stella had curly red hair, Kate was tall, with her blonde hair cut in a blunt bob, and Issie had long dark hair and olive skin, just like her mum.

"But inside, where it counts, you girls are identical," Mrs Brown would say. "You're all utterly horse-mad!"

It was a short drive from the River Paddock to the pony-club grounds. Avery was up front driving and the three girls sat in the cabin of the horse truck together. Behind them, in the very rear of the truck, were the horses. Comet, Toby and Marmite were all tied up in their partitions with a hay net each and the girls only had to open the back cabin door to walk through and check on them. Not that they really needed to, as the drive to the pony club was a brief ten minutes up the road.

"I can't believe there's just one more week of school," Stella was saying. "Remember this time last year when we were all going to Blackthorn Farm to help Hester with the riding school?"

The three of them had been keen to go back to Gisborne and help out again this year too, but Issie's Aunt Hester had decided not to open the school this summer. Her business, training movie stunt horses, was booming right now, and she had so much work on she couldn't do both at once. That meant the girls were on the lookout for new holiday jobs.

As they unloaded the horses from the truck, Issie grabbed Comet's tack. She had decided to ride the skewbald at the rally today because she knew they'd be doing lots of showjumping. Her other horse, Blaze, was a good jumper too, but was really best at dressage. The chestnut Anglo-Arab mare had once belonged to the famed El Caballo Danza Magnifico riding school in Spain, and Blaze's son, Issie's beloved colt Nightstorm, was there right now, about to begin his dressage training, just as his mother had done before him.

Comet, on the other hand, was no dressage horse. He got bored schooling – and let Issie know it by doing a cheerful buck if she tried to spend too much time on flatwork. Comet was a true showjumper and he was happiest when he was in the competition ring, showing off his style to the crowd as he flew over fences that were bigger than he was!

Comet's jumping prowess could be a problem sometimes. Issie would often turn up at the River Paddock to find him in a different field from the one he'd been put in the night before. No fence could hold Comet. Issie remembered the very first time she met the cheeky skewbald, he had jumped out of his paddock and almost collided with Aunt Hester's horse truck!

Hester had been driven mad by Comet's antics when he lived at Blackthorn Farm. When Issie entered him in the Horse of the Year Show, Comet finally put his jumping ability to good use. His spectacular performance in the puissance won them prize money, and attracted the attention of celebrity showjumping trainer Ginty McLintoch, who offered to buy the skewbald on the spot!

But Hester had refused Ginty's offer and given Comet to Issie instead. Ever since then, whenever Issie bumped into Ginty at showjumping events the flame-haired trainer always repeated her offer to buy the skewbald.

Ginty ran private stables in Chevalier Point where she schooled horses for wealthy clients and also ran a string of competitive showjumpers. Natasha Tucker was one of Ginty's clients. The sour-faced blonde always made a point of telling the other Chevalier Point riders how brilliant her private lessons were. The way Natasha told it, Ginty was a proper instructor and would never waste her time with a bunch of useless pony-club kids the way Tom Avery did.

Ginty certainly had a reputation for being too posh for pony club. The one place Issie never expected to see Ginty was at a Chevalier Point rally day. So when she spotted the trainer standing over by Natasha's horse truck talking with Mrs Tucker, she was utterly amazed.

"What's she doing here?" Issie whispered to Stella and Kate. The three girls were all staring when Ginty suddenly turned round and caught them ogling at her. Surprisingly, the haughty redhead gave them a wave.

"Ohmygod!" Stella said. "She's coming over."

Ginty was striding across the paddocks with a determined look on her face. Her gaze was set on Issie and Comet. She had obviously recognised the skewbald pony and was homing in for a closer look.

"Good morning, girls," Ginty said briskly. "Lovely day for riding!" Having dispensed with the pleasantries, she focused her attention on Issie. "How is Comet doing? Have you changed your mind about selling him to me yet?"

"He's doing just fine," Issie replied, "but he's still not for sale."

"I see," Ginty said. "Well, I've got a couple of gaps in my team that I'm trying to fill this week before the competition season gets underway. You know where to find me if you change your mind."

She presented a business card to Issie with her name

and number on it, then turned on her heel and headed
back to the Tuckers' horse truck. The conversation was
clearly over.

Tom Avery started the rally the same way he always
did, with a gear inspection. There were over fifty club
members present that morning, and after Avery had
worked down the row, checking stirrup leathers and
tutting over dirty bits and loose girths, he divided the
ride up into four. The junior members were assigned
their instructors and sent off to various training areas.
Only the most senior Chevalier Point members stayed
with Avery in the jumping ring.

There were eight of them. Issie, Stella and Kate were
joined by their friends Dan, Ben, Annabel and Morgan,
and Natasha Tucker was there too on Romeo.

As a warm-up exercise, Avery had set up four jumps,
positioned around the arena in a circle at three, six, nine
and twelve o'clock.

"They're not very big, are they?" Dan said with
disappointment as he eyed up the jumps. The four

fences were quite low, no more than half a metre off the ground.

"We'll begin at this height as a warm-up," Avery told him. "It doesn't matter what size the fence is, I'm looking for good technique from all of you. You're going to canter in a circle over the jumps, making sure you keep the rhythm steady between fences and aim for the centre of each jump."

As the riders rode around the course, Avery focused on correcting their positions. He was particularly keen to observe how well they executed their crest release, making sure that they eased the reins up the neck at the moment the horse took off, giving their mounts enough freedom to stretch out in an arc over the jumps.

"Don't just fling the reins at him, Stella!" Avery called out. "The release should be smooth."

"Slow down his canter by sitting back between fences, Natasha," Avery instructed.

Natasha didn't look happy to be given advice. She glared at Avery, and then looked over to Ginty, who was leaning against the rails at the sideline watching the riders closely. Ginty's eyes weren't trained on Romeo, though. She was watching Comet. When Avery raised the rails of the fences to a substantial one metre high, Ginty couldn't take her eyes off the skewbald as he jumped each fence cleanly and perfectly, taking off neatly at exactly the right time and maintaining a rhythmic canter stride all the way around the ring.

When the riders had finished their training for the morning, Issie could have sworn Ginty was still watching as she rode out of the arena, but by the time she had tied Comet up to the horse truck, the trainer wasn't anywhere to be seen. Natasha was at her horse truck unsaddling Romeo, but Ginty had disappeared.

It had only been a rally day, but Issie was still thrilled with Comet's performance. "You should have seen the way he took the oxer," she told her mum as they drove home.

"What's an oxer?" Mrs Brown said. Issie sighed. Her mum knew nothing about horses or riding. Issie was used to it by now, and she had long ago got over her envy for riders like Morgan Chatswood-Smith who had horsey parents. OK, maybe her mum wasn't horsey, but

Issie was grateful that she had always supported her. She must have spent a fortune over the years on farriers and feed bills, lessons and grazing.

Mrs Brown even understood when Issie had to go to Spain to try and get Nightstorm back when the colt was stolen. So it must have been with serious consideration that she began the conversation in the car that day.

"Issie," she said, "I've been thinking about your school report."

Issie groaned. "Oh Mum, I get it, OK? You're proud of me. That's great. Can we move on?"

Mrs Brown shook her head. "I think this report proves what you are capable of. You're growing up so fast. Next year you'll be in the fifth form and it's time that you started thinking about the future. What do you plan to do with your life?"

"You know that already, Mum," Issie said. "I want to ride horses. That's all I've ever wanted."

"Yes, I know," Mrs Brown said in a measured voice, "but Issie, that's not a proper job, is it? Riding horses is something you love doing, but you need to think about what you are going to do with your life... as a career."

"But I've already decided," Issie frowned. "I'm going to be a competitive horse rider."

"Sweetie, I think you need to be realistic," Mrs Brown said. "What are the chances of you making a living that way? That's why school is so important. If you continue to get marks like your last report, you could be anything you want to be. I've already put aside a university fund for you, so that's not a problem. You just need a bit of solid workplace experience so you can think about what career you should focus on..." she took a deep breath. "I made a phone call today while you were at the pony club, and spoke to David, one of the partners at my office."

Mrs Brown worked as a legal secretary for a large law firm in town. She had been part-time when Issie was little, but after Issie's dad had moved away when she was nine, Mrs Brown began working full-time to make ends meet. Issie sometimes went to the office after school to meet her mum instead of going straight home. The partners at the law firm were always nice to her, although she couldn't really tell any of them apart. They were all tall men in dark grey suits with bald heads, polite smiles and very firm handshakes.

"Anyway, I told David about your latest school report," Mrs Brown continued, "and he's very kindly agreed that you can do work experience at the firm for the whole of the holidays. They'll even pay you an hourly rate – it's not much, but really it's the experience that counts."

"What?" Issie couldn't believe it. "But I don't want to work at your office!"

"Issie, this is a great opportunity," Mrs Brown insisted.

"I can't believe this is my punishment for getting a good school report!"

"Don't be ridiculous, Isadora," her mother said firmly.

"Well, it feels like that!" Issie couldn't help herself. "It's not fair!"

"Issie! You said yourself that you needed a holiday job."

"But I don't want to be stuck in some stuffy office!"

Mrs Brown was taken aback. "It's not stuffy. We have excellent air conditioning."

"You know what I mean."

"Beggars can't be choosers," her mum pointed out. "You only have a week until holidays start and you haven't found anything else yet."

"But I—"

Mrs Brown was exasperated. "Either you come up with a magical job offer where someone is actually willing to pay you to ride ponies all day, or you will be coming to work with me at the law firm next week when school finishes."

There was silence in the car. You could have cut the air with a knife. Finally, Mrs Brown spoke again, her voice calm and softer this time. "You're fifteen years old, Issie. Maybe it's time to grow up. Horses are all well and good, but they are not a real job. I'm thinking about your future."

"Me too," Issie muttered.

What else was there to say? Issie could see the future that her mother had planned for her. And there wasn't a single horse in it.

Chapter 2

Issie had been planning to give Comet the day off after the rally and spend Sunday morning hacking out on Blaze, but her mum had other ideas.

"You need some nice clothes to wear to the office next week," Mrs Brown insisted. And so, instead of going riding, Issie spent Sunday morning being dragged around the shops while her mother bought her a smart black skirt, a striped cotton dress, two blouses and a pair of chic black ballet pumps.

"I don't see why we're doing this," Issie grumbled as Mrs Brown handed her credit card over the counter at the shoe store.

"Because you can't wear riding boots and jods to

work at a law firm," Mrs Brown told her. "Now, how about we get you a nice jacket as well?"

By the time the shopping torture was over half the day was already gone. Issie still had time to ride, but she decided it was too late to hack out, so she'd focus on dressage instead.

The dark cloud that had been hanging over her all morning disappeared when she saw Blaze waiting for her at the River Paddock gate. It was hard to stay in a bad mood when you were with a horse, especially one as beautiful as Blaze.

With her flaxen mane and tail, white socks and deep liver chestnut coat, Blaze was the prettiest horse you could imagine. Her delicate beauty was the result of centuries of breeding and she had once been the most prized mare of El Caballo Danza Magnifico. However, Issie hadn't known anything about her pony's incredible history when they first met.

Blaze had been in a terrible state, mistreated and abused, filthy and half-starved, when Tom Avery turned up with her three years ago in his horse truck. Chevalier Point's head instructor worked for Horse Welfare and it was his job to re-home rescued horses. Initially, Issie was wary. She wanted to help but she was still recovering from the horrific loss of her own pony, her beloved dapple-grey Mystic, who had been killed in a terrible accident.

One look at Blaze, however, convinced Issie that she had no choice. This mare really needed her. Together the heartbroken girl and the pony began to heal each other.

Through it all though, Issie had never forgotten Mystic. She still loved the grey pony and she felt as if somehow he was still there with her.

It turned out she was right. There was a connection between Issie and her pony that was too strong to be broken. Mystic returned to Issie, not like a ghost, but as real as any horse, flesh and blood at her side ready to help her, whenever she really needed him.

Mystic had helped Issie so many times. They had ridden together in the middle of the night to catch saboteurs and horse thieves, and taken wild rides in broad daylight to save the Blackthorn Ponies in the Gisborne high country. But a couple of months ago when Issie had been riding at the Young Rider Challenge in Australia, Issie had begun to doubt her special bond with the grey pony. There were moments when she thought he had abandoned her. Things had got really desperate and it had become a constant fear that she would inevitably lose her bond with Mystic, as his appearances seemed less frequent as time passed. But Mystic had come through in the end in Australia, turning up when she truly needed him, just as he always did. And although she saw him less and less, she knew that Mystic wouldn't leave her. He had never let her down, he was her protector.

But now a new threat loomed over Issie – one that Mystic couldn't prevent. After so many adventures together, was this how it would end? Not in some wild, dangerous escapade, but with Issie stuck in the offices of some boring law firm? Not even Mystic could save her from Mrs Brown's awful plan, which would keep her inside and away from horses for the whole holidays!

Issie tried to stop thinking about the stupid holiday job. She had almost finished grooming and tacking up Blaze, and as she did up the last straps on the cavesson and the throat lash, she was determined to make the most of her ride. After all, she wasn't going to have much riding time left this summer if she was working from nine to five.

As they entered the arena, Issie rode Blaze on a loose rein to stretch her neck out long and low, and then gradually collected her up, doing lots of trot transitions before cantering in half circles to change the rein.

She had been working lately on the mare's lateral work – which meant fancy dressage moves like half-passes and shoulder-ins. Blaze had been well-schooled in all these manoeuvres a long time ago when she was with El Caballo Danza Magnifico, so it was just a matter of pressing the right buttons and the mare would break out the most magnificent dressage paces.

Issie had been riding for nearly an hour and was just finishing up with some trot serpentines when she realised that there was a figure standing beside the arena, watching her. Startled, she pulled Blaze up to a halt.

"Don't stop on my account!" the woman called out. "I was quite happy watching you. I've been here for ages. She's a beautiful mare, isn't she?"

The woman stepped over the side barrier of the arena and strode over towards Issie. She was wearing khaki jodhpurs and a white polo shirt. Issie hadn't recognised her at first because she was wearing a cap on top of her flame-red hair and a pair of wraparound sunglasses hid her eyes.

"I called at your house and your mum said I would find you here," Ginty McLintoch said. "I hope it's OK, turning up like this? I didn't mean to interrupt your training."

"That's OK," Issie said. "Blaze and I were nearly finished anyway."

Ginty nodded. "So this is your other pony?" She ran a cool, professional eye over Blaze, examining her conformation. "She's certainly a looker. Does she jump?"

Issie felt herself stiffen at the question. "She's not for sale either," Issie said. "I got given her, and it's a really long story… but I would never sell her."

Issie couldn't believe the nerve! Ginty had failed to buy Comet, so why would she ever think that Issie was willing to sell Blaze?

"I think I've given you the wrong end of the stick," Ginty said hastily, sensing Issie's hostility. "I'm not trying to buy your mare. Don't get me wrong. She's very nice, but I really didn't come here to talk about your ponies."

Issie was confused. "Then what are you here for?"

Ginty looked at her with a serious expression. "You," she said. "I'm here for you, Issie. I want to offer you a job at my stables."

Ginty McLintoch didn't mess around when it came to business. Her discussion with Issie was swift and simple. She had a place in her stables over the school holidays for a junior groom. She was looking for a young rider who knew their way around a showjumper and could handle the responsibilities of exercising, feeding and grooming up to six horses a day.

"The pay isn't great and the hours are long," Ginty conceded, "but you will get to ride some fantastic horses. Not only every day for basic training, but also at competitions on the circuit. I guarantee you'll learn more about riding in seven weeks with me than you've probably learnt in all the years you've been taught by Tom Avery."

There was a sneer in Ginty's voice as she said Avery's name. Issie was well aware that the flame-haired trainer frowned upon Avery's methods. Natasha Tucker was always talking about the rivalry between them. Ginty considered Chevalier Point Pony Club's head instructor a low-powered amateur, compared to her and the high-stakes world of professional paid riders.

The dislike was mutual. Avery had made it quite clear that he was not a fan of Ginty's methods either. Issie had heard him complaining about the slew of bad habits that Ginty had taught her star pupil, Natasha Tucker. The spoilt blonde was rather too fond of relying on her whip and was renowned for her 'busy' hands. But was that really Ginty's doing?

Ginty obviously liked the way Issie handled her horses – otherwise surely she wouldn't have offered her the job? And if Ginty thought that Issie was a good rider then perhaps her methods weren't a world away from Avery's after all.

Ginty was a famous trainer. She had brought on more than her fair share of champions. And being a junior groom in Ginty's stables meant the chance to spend the school holidays riding amazing horses every day, instead of helping her mum with filing bits of paper and getting the lawyers cups of tea!

"Would I still have time to ride my own horses?" Issie asked.

"That's up to you," Ginty replied. "You'll be working a six-day week – sometimes seven days when we're competing at the shows. You'll start at seven each morning and sometimes we'll be away for days at a time on the show circuit, but usually if you're not too exhausted by the time you finish work at four, then you'll have time left at the end of the day to ride your own horses."

"It sounds brilliant, thank you," Issie said politely, "but I need to think about it."

"Well, you don't have much time to do that, I'm afraid," Ginty said. "I need an answer soon. I've only got a week to find someone and I can't afford to sit on my hands. Tell me now if you're not keen, because I have a couple of other riders that I'm considering."

"No!" Issie said hastily. "I mean, yes. Don't offer anyone else the job. I want to do it. I just need to go home and check with my mum…"

Issie spent the bike ride home rehearsing the best way of breaking the news to her mother. She had a well-prepared little speech all ready, but instantly forgot it the minute she walked in the door.

"Ginty McLintoch has offered me a job. You said I'd

never find a job with horses, but I have, and I want to go and work for her."

Some people would call the conversation that followed an argument. Later on, when she had calmed down, Mrs Brown referred to it as a 'heated discussion'. In the end, though, Issie didn't care what her mum called it. She had won. Mrs Brown finally conceded defeat. After all, she had told her daughter that if she could find herself a paid job with ponies, then she could take it.

"On the plus side," Mrs Brown reasoned, "starting work at seven each morning and mucking out poo from that many loose boxes every day might finally make you think about getting qualifications for a proper career. I know I'd rather be sitting down with a cup of tea in a nice air-conditioned office than doing back-breaking work at a stable any day."

This was the difference between her and her mother. Issie would rather be sweating in the stables for a pittance. Horses were her dream job and she had just been given her big break.

Stella and Kate couldn't believe it when Issie told them her news at school the next day.

"You are soooo lucky!" Stella breathed excitedly. "I am so jealous! Ginty was really watching *you* at the pony club that day, when you thought she just wanted to buy Comet! Do you think she needs any more riders?"

Stella's holiday job was restocking the shelves each night at the local supermarket, and she wasn't thrilled with it. "We have to wear smocks and hairnets," she groaned. "It's going to be awful."

"Have you told Tom yet?" Kate asked.

"No." Issie shook her head. "I'm going to Winterflood Farm tomorrow after school to help out with a new rescue pony that he's just brought in. I thought I would tell him then."

"I thought Tom didn't like Ginty?" Stella said.

"He doesn't," Issie admitted, "but when I explain to him how I didn't really have a choice, I'm sure he'll be OK about it."

She was dead wrong.

"You can't work for Ginty," Avery told her point blank when she broke the news.

"But Tom, if I don't take the job Mum will make me spend the holidays at her office and I won't get to ride at all—"

"Anything is better than working for that atrocious woman," Avery said.

"Why?" Issie was confused. "I know Ginty has different methods from you—"

"You've got no idea!" Avery said, clearly refusing to back down. "Issie, you don't understand the pressure you'll be under riding for Dulmoth Park. Ginty's got financial backers with big wallets and huge expectations. It's all about making money for her, and she's willing to do whatever it takes to win."

"So she's competitive. There's nothing wrong with that," Issie insisted. "I know it's a big step for me, working at a professional stables, but I can handle myself. Besides, when we were in Australia a couple of months ago you were willing to let me move to Kentucky to go to Blainford. Now I've got a holiday job and you're acting like it's a big deal!"

"This is different," Avery said coolly. "Tara Kelly is a brilliant trainer and Blainford Academy is the best riding institution in the world. I was only doing what was best for you—"

"I'm fifteen years old!" Issie objected. "I'm not a kid any more, and you need to stop deciding what's best for me! You're not my dad, you know. You're just my pony-club instructor!"

The words came out before Issie could stop them. And then she saw the pain in Avery's eyes, deep disappointment written all over his face.

"Tom," Issie stammered, "I'm… I'm sorry. I didn't mean…"

"It's OK," Avery said quietly. "And you're right, this is your decision. I can't make your mind up for you. Maybe it's time for you to try a new instructor. Maybe this is a good thing."

And with that he turned his back on Issie and headed towards the stable block.

"Tom?" Issie called running after him. "Wait… I thought you wanted me to help with the new pony?"

Avery turned back to look at her. "No, Issie, I think

it's probably best if you go home. I can cope with the pony on my own."

In all the time she had known Tom Avery, Issie had never heard such hurt in her instructor's voice. As she watched him walk away, she wondered whether she was really doing the right thing. But it was too late to change her mind now. She had already told Ginty that she would take the job. She was starting work at Dulmoth Park on Monday.

Chapter 3

Issie stared up at the horse towering above her. It was rearing up on its hind legs, with a tousled mane and wild eyes. She put a hand out to stroke the horse and felt cool, smooth marble against her skin. There was the security keypad, embedded in the pedestal below the statue, just as Ginty had described it. The letters on the pad lit up bright blue at the touch of her fingertips as she carefully coded in the password Ginty had given her – w-i-n-n-e-r.

The sleek, state-of-the-art metal gates beside the statue slid open and Issie wheeled her bike through the grand entrance and into the manicured grounds of Dulmoth Park.

Issie had got up at 6 a.m. to make it to work on time. She had dressed, eaten breakfast and then cycled the half-hour journey along the main road past the pony club and the Chevalier Point airfield to reach the stables. She had hoped that maybe her mum would drive her to work, but Mrs Brown had laughed when Issie suggested this.

"You want me to drive you to work before seven?" Her mum was horrified. "You must be joking! I'm not getting up at dawn each day to be a taxi service."

It had been hard to force herself out of bed, but once she was up and on her bike, Issie actually enjoyed the ride to the stables. The morning air was crisp, and as she cycled up the driveway of Dulmoth Park the grounds looked pristine and perfect with the dawn light tinting everything golden.

As she rode past the white post and rail fences, Issie noticed that Dulmoth Park's paddocks were eerily empty. There were no horses grazing. Even in summer, when New Zealand nights were warm and most horses were left out to pasture, Ginty had a reputation for keeping her horses stabled. Right now the horses would still be tucked up snugly in their loose boxes, waiting for their day to start.

The stable complex at the end of the long driveway had the air of a posh racehorse training facility. The driveway forked in three directions and there was a series of smart, creosoted black buildings surrounded by well-pruned trees and neat lawns.

Issie had just dismounted from her bike and was wondering which path to take when suddenly two very yappy, angry-looking Jack Russells came charging out from the building right in front of her.

The dogs were barking their heads off as they bore down on her. They were just a few feet away and closing in fast when a sharp whistle made them stop in their tracks.

"Hoi! Jock! Angus!" Ginty McLintoch called out.

At the sound of Ginty's voice Jock and Angus sat down obediently, waiting for their mistress to catch up.

"I'm sorry about that," Ginty said. "They're very suspicious of strangers." She smiled at Issie. "They'll be fine now that they can see you're with me."

Issie put out her hands to scratch the two Jack Russells under the chin. "Hi Jock, hi Angus!" She smiled at Ginty. "I love dogs. I've got a blue heeler at home."

"A blue heeler?"

"An Australian cattle dog," Issie explained.

"Good around horses?" Ginty asked.

"Wombat's brilliant with horses."

"Wombat?" Ginty was confused. "I thought you said he was a dog?"

"He is a dog," Issie said. "His name is Wombat. I got him in Australia… it's kind of a long story."

"Well," Ginty said briskly, clearly not interested in hearing it, "as long as he doesn't bother the horses and he can put up with Jock and Angus, then you're welcome to bring him to work with you."

"Really?" Issie couldn't believe it. "That would be amazing!"

"You can park your bike in the equipment room," Ginty told her. "It's just through that doorway beside the office." She looked at her watch. "I'd better go down to the stables. I've got another new junior groom starting today as well. Come and join us there when you're ready."

The equipment room was stocked with jump stands and painted rails. Issie leant her bike against the wall and unzipped her backpack. She'd already put her helmet on for the bike ride and she grabbed her back protector out of the backpack and slipped it on too before heading for the stable block.

Up ahead of her at the stable entrance Ginty was engrossed in conversation with two girls who looked a couple of years older than Issie. They were both dressed exactly the same, in smart cream jodhpurs, work boots and dark purple sweatshirts with the letters *DP* embroidered on them in swirly gold. The *DP* obviously stood for Dulmoth Park.

"Issie," Ginty called out, "come and meet my senior grooms."

The two girls looked up at Issie and the one with freckles and honey-coloured hair in a ponytail gave her a warm smile.

"Hi!" The honey-blonde gave a wave. "I'm Penny."

The girl next to Penny had brown hair cut in a short pixie crop. She didn't smile or say hello, she just stared at Issie suspiciously.

"This is Verity – my head groom," Ginty said, taking over on the introductions since Verity clearly wasn't going to introduce herself. "Verity and Penny have both been with me for two seasons already, so they know the ropes," Ginty continued. "I've asked Verity to assign you and Natasha your work rosters. You'll find details on the blackboard just inside the front door of the stables…"

Issie froze. Did Ginty just say *Natasha*? No, it couldn't be…

At that moment the gates to Dulmoth Park slid open and a silver Mercedes glided down the driveway. Issie recognised the car straight away, and the sour-faced blonde sitting inside it.

Natasha Tucker emerged from the passenger seat looking utterly miserable, grabbed her bag, muttered a dismissive goodbye to her mother and then slammed the Mercedes door shut. She glared after the car as Mrs Tucker drove off again.

"Good morning, Natasha." Ginty smiled at her. "I believe I told you it was a 7 a.m. start, so let's try to be on time in future."

"Whatever!" Natasha groaned.

Issie would never have spoken to Ginty like that, but the trainer seemed to let Natasha get away with it. She ignored the comment and continued, "I was just doing introductions. You know Verity and Penny already, and I'm sure you know Isadora too?"

"We go to pony club together," Natasha confirmed, looking far from pleased to see Issie.

"I've just been explaining the roster," Ginty said. "Verity will organise it so that you and Isadora are each in charge of six horses. You'll need to do all the feeds and have the first horse ready in the arena by eight each morning to begin schooling. Everything is written down for you on the blackboards in the tack room, but if you have any questions about the way we do things here, then check with Verity."

This clearly didn't sit well with the head groom, who didn't seem keen on answering any questions. She was already edging towards the stables, trying to get away. "Can I go now?" she asked. "I've still got to sort out Tottie and Flame's hard feeds. We're already running late."

Ginty nodded. "Take Issie with you to help."

Verity grunted, and Issie figured that must mean she should follow as the head groom set off towards the far end of the stables.

The feed room was nothing like the tatty old tack

shed where the feed was stored at Winterflood Farm. This room looked like a science lab – or a pharmacy. Large feed lockers with airtight lids lined one side of the room and above these were shelves filled with a mind-boggling array of powders, additives and supplements.

Verity seemed to know exactly what each of the bottles contained. She had grabbed a feed bin and was busily throwing in various measures from different bottles and tubs on the shelves.

"We're trying to put more condition on Tottie at the moment," Verity said. "I've been giving her two scoops of boiled barley in her feed morning and night, plus one of chaff and one of Maxi-equine hi-performance, and we add linseed, magnesium and electrolytes to each meal. Plus I've been putting in selenium lately as well."

Now she grabbed a second feed bin and began to pour out measures and doses of potions off the shelf. "Flame's on three scoops of the Maxi-equine, plus the chaff and supplements and extra potassium," Verity continued.

"I don't think I can remember all of this," Issie murmured, feeling quite ill at the thought of giving the horses the wrong dose or muddling the feeds up entirely.

"You don't have to learn it off by heart. Just look at the chart on the wall," Verity said. "It gives you feed instructions for every horse in the stables."

Issie noticed that there was one feed locker that Verity didn't use at all. It wasn't a round tub like the rest – it was low and square, standing in the corner of the room. Its lid was curved and inlaid with metal and it was bolted shut like a treasure chest with a combination lock on the outside of it.

"What's in that one?" Issie asked.

Verity stiffened. "Medicines… stuff for emergencies," she said, adding bluntly, "Leave it alone. You don't need to worry about it."

She finished stirring the feeds using a huge wooden spoon, and then passed one of the big buckets to Issie.

"You can give Flame his feed. He's in the stall at the end on your left."

As Issie approached Flame's loose box, she could hear the horse stamping about inside, pacing and whinnying impatiently as he heard her coming closer. Both the top and bottom half of the Dutch door were shut tight and

Issie wondered what the horse on the other side looked like. All she knew was that with a name like Flame he had to be a chestnut.

When she swung the door open, she was amazed. Flame's coat was like nothing she had ever seen before. It shone like a newly minted copper coin. He had the most athletic conformation Issie had ever seen, with muscles and sinew rippling as he moved about restlessly in his stall.

Flame was clearly expecting his breakfast. He stomped and nickered, impatiently waiting for Issie to unbolt the door, and then made a beeline for her as she entered the stall. With the feed bin propped under one arm, she had to use the other hand to fend him off, moving quickly through the loose box to deftly slide the bin into the wallfeeder slot at the far end.

As Flame happily snuffled down his feed, Issie was free to stand back and assess the gelding more thoroughly. She guessed that he was around sixteen hands high, but his imposing presence made him seem much bigger than that. He wasn't a fine-boned Thoroughbred but a heavier breed, perhaps some kind of warmblood or a Selle Francais like Natasha's chestnut, Romeo. His shoulders and neck were powerful, and although his hindquarters were well developed his withers were still higher than his rump, which indicated that his power was in his front half, a classic sign of a horse that had been bred to jump. He had an elegant, refined head and thoughtful deep brown eyes. His bold chestnut colour made a striking contrast with the pretty white star on the gelding's forehead and the white snip on his muzzle.

"You're really gorgeous!" Issie breathed out loud.

"He should be!"

It was Verity, leaning over the partition of the Dutch door and looking at Flame. "He cost a fortune and it was a total drama getting him here. He had to be imported from Europe. His bloodlines are amazing – he's by Brilliant Fire."

Issie looked blankly at her.

"You mean you haven't heard of Brilliant Fire?" Verity sighed dramatically at this. "He's a Hanoverian stallion, a warmblood from Germany. Brilliant Fire has sired more Olympic showjumpers than any other stallion. All of his progeny – his sons and daughters – are worth a fortune because of their bloodlines."

"So how much did Ginty pay for Flame?" Issie asked.

"Oh, Ginty didn't buy him!" Verity said, looking at Issie as if she were the most naïve person on the planet. "Ginty could never afford him – or any of the other horses here for that matter."

"You mean she doesn't own any of the horses?" Issie was confused.

"She doesn't even own Dulmoth Park!" Verity said. "Ginty's in charge, but she's not the one with the money. Cassandra Steele, you know, the millionairess? She owns the stables and most of the horses. Ginty also stables a few 'weekend rides' for clients with loads of money and no time. Ginty keeps their horses for them here at an exorbitant cost. It's a total luxury – some of the clients only ride their horses once a month. Imagine having your own horse and only bothering to ride it twelve times a year!"

"Don't the horses go bonkers if there's no one riding them?" Issie asked.

"Oh, we ride them," Verity said. "Ginty charges even more money for that. Penny and I exercise the horses on the owner's behalf so that they're kept in regular work."

"You're so lucky. It must be amazing, being paid to ride really fab horses every day."

Verity looked at Issie as if she were an idiot. "The owners have high expectations. It's up to us to make them happy," she said flatly. "It costs a fortune to keep your horse at Dulmoth Park, but the rich ladies love it, because it's so exclusive and Ginty treats them all like rock stars. We keep their horses fit and do everything for them. Ginty always says that her clients pay top dollar so that they can step out of their car and get straight on to their horse."

Issie thought about all those times Natasha had turned up at rally days with Romeo immaculately groomed and plaited – quite boastful about having done none of the work herself. No doubt Penny and Verity were the ones who did it for her.

"Why is Natasha working here?" Issie asked. "She's one of Ginty's clients, isn't she?"

Verity shrugged. "Her dad has some sort of money trouble. Ginty says it's only temporary. He's a big-deal property developer and a deal fell through. Natasha's parents are making her work here for the holidays to cover the cost of her horse's board, otherwise Ginty wouldn't be able to keep stabling Romeo."

Issie knew exactly what 'trouble' Mr Tucker had

got himself into. In fact, Issie was the one who had uncovered his dodgy business dealings while she competed on Fortune to win the Golden Trophy! It was ironic, Issie thought, that she should end up stuck with Natasha for the school holidays – and in a strange way it was her own fault!

"Ginty still sucks up to the Tuckers because of their money," Verity continued. "You saw the way she treated Natasha, letting her arrive late this morning. The rest of us would have been hung, drawn and quartered…" Verity stopped in mid-sentence. "I'm sorry. I shouldn't be talking to you like this. You and Natasha both go to the same pony club, don't you? You're probably best friends."

Issie gave a hollow laugh. "Hardly! Natasha can't stand me!"

Verity looked surprised at this. "Really? I thought you were… You know, you have to be careful," she said darkly, "you never know who your friends are around here…"

Verity looked like she was about to say something else, but Issie never found out what, because at that moment Ginty suddenly appeared beside her at the stall door.

"Come on!" the trainer said briskly. "Morning exercise is already behind schedule, we don't have time to stand around chatting."

"I better go get Tottie ready," Verity said to Issie. "Check the blackboard roster to see which horse you're working first. I'll see you in the arena."

Issie found the blackboard on the back of the door in the tack room. Riders' names were listed along the top of the board with the horses they were assigned written down underneath. Issie noted with disappointment that Flame had been given to Natasha. She had been hoping that she would be the one to ride the big chestnut. Penny was down to ride Vertigo, and Verity was supposed to ride a horse called Tottenham Hotspur, which Issie figured must be Tottie's show name. The first horse on Issie's list was "Tokyo". Issie searched through the saddle racks fixed to the wall and found Tokyo's name plate with a saddle, bridle and numnah.

Tokyo's saddle was made from warm honey-coloured leather, finished with orange stitching and a single word stamped elegantly into the flap at the front: *Hermès*.

Issie was almost scared to touch it. She had never seen a real Hermès saddle before – they were worth thousands and thousands of dollars. And now she was going to ride in one!

Picking Tokyo's saddle up carefully, she carried it with the numnah over her arm and the bridle slung on her left shoulder, back out into the stable corridor. It wasn't until she was standing there looking at the row of stalls that she realised there was a problem. The loose boxes didn't have name plates. How was she supposed to find her horse?

Still carrying the gear, she strode down the corridor towards the end stall. Verity would be in there saddling up Tottie. She could tell Issie which stall held Tokyo.

The door to Tottie's loose box was unlocked, so Issie pushed it open and walked straight in to see Verity standing alongside a nervous-looking dapple-grey mare. Verity was bent down over the horse's hocks. Her right hand was gripping a hypodermic syringe.

As she held the syringe aloft, Verity's face was tight with determination. She took aim, and then with all her strength she hammered her fist down hard, forcing the hypodermic needle deep into the upper muscle of the horse's hind leg.

"Verity! What are you doing?" Issie cried out. But it

was too late. Verity had already pushed down the plunger of the syringe and injected the contents of the hypodermic into Tottie.

With a quick yank, she pulled the needle back out again, capped the empty syringe and then she slipped it into her pocket. She let the mare go and walked over to Issie.

"Verity," Issie said, "what was that?"

The head groom raised a finger to her lips. "Say nothing about this," she warned. "Trust me. If you know what's good for you, you don't want to get involved."

Verity's face was stony as she pushed past Issie in the doorway. Then she turned round and added bitterly, "Welcome to Dulmoth Park, Issie. You really have no idea what you're in for."

Chapter 4

Issie was still shaking with shock when she stepped out into the corridor a few moments later and bumped right into Penny, almost knocking her over.

"Sorry!" Issie squeaked.

"It's all right," Penny insisted. Then she saw the startled look on Issie's face. "Are you OK?"

"I'm... I'm trying to find Tokyo," Issie stammered. "Do you know which stall I'm looking for?" She wanted to tell Penny about what she'd just seen, but Verity's warning made her think twice – after all, she still had no idea who to trust in this place.

"She's in the third stall up there on your right," Penny said.

Tokyo turned out to be a very pretty bright bay mare with black stockings and a white star on her forehead. At seventeen hands high the mare towered over Issie, and she had to lead her over to the mounting block at the arena entrance to get up high enough to put her foot in the stirrup and climb on.

Natasha was already in the arena when Issie rode Tokyo in. Natasha was mounted up on a bay as well. He was much darker than Tokyo, and smaller too, a neatly put-together Thoroughbred whose name turned out to be Sebastian.

Issie had been expecting Penny and Verity to be riding with them as well, but instead the two senior grooms were on foot, standing like sentries on either side of the single upright rail in the middle of the arena.

"Right! This morning is already running behind schedule. Let's get started," Ginty said. She looked at Issie. "We're going to be doing rapping today. Have you done it before?"

Issie frowned. "You mean, like, singing with hip-hop music?"

Natasha let out a gleeful snort. "Rapping is a jumping technique. I thought everybody knew that!"

"Natasha has done it before, of course," Ginty smiled indulgently at her pupil. "Since she's already familiar with my methods, it's probably best if she goes first to show you how it's done."

Ginty instructed Natasha to take Sebastian to the other end of the arena. "Get him into a canter and then bring him back over the jump," she told her.

"Aren't we doing flatwork exercises first?" Issie couldn't help asking. She was used to doing dressage as a warm-up with Avery before their jumping sessions, but Ginty clearly had different ideas.

"They're showjumpers, not *haute école* schoolmasters," she said dismissively. "They don't need to warm up."

Issie didn't say anything more. She sat on Tokyo and kept her eyes on Natasha as she turned Sebastian and rode him in hard towards the upright rail.

"Use your stick!" Ginty instructed. Natasha already had her whip raised, and gave the horse two solid thwacks with her riding crop right in front of the jump.

At the touch of the whip, Sebastian leapt. Issie could see straight away that he was an athletic jumper. The gelding lifted his front legs up neatly and began his arc.

He would have cleared the rail easily – if it weren't for Penny and Verity.

At the exact moment that Sebastian took off, the two girls positioned on either side of the jump both grasped on to an end of the top rail. They waited until Sebastian had his front legs over the jump and then they lifted the rail out of its cups and quickly hoisted it up another twenty centimetres in the air.

Sebastian didn't know that the rail had been raised, or that his hind legs were no longer lifted high enough to make it over the jump. He bashed both fetlocks hard against the painted pole. Issie could hear the crunch of bone scraping the wood as Sebastian literally didn't know what hit him. He landed on the other side of the jump looking quite shaken and bolted forward to get away.

Natasha was prepared for his reaction. She yanked hard on the reins to pull him back and then brought the dark bay gelding around to rejoin the others. She had a smile on her face as she rode back towards Ginty. "Good, Natasha!" Ginty said. Then she turned to Issie. "That's how it's done. Your turn!"

Issie was stunned. "Are they going to lift the rail when I jump too?"

"That's the plan," Ginty confirmed.

"But Tokyo will hit it!" Issie didn't understand.

"That's the point," Ginty told her. "If the horses lift their legs up high enough, they won't hit the rail."

"But the horses don't know that the rail is being moved."

"Not at first," Ginty agreed, "but after they get a few bangs they exaggerate their leg lift and soon they're clearing the rail with room to spare. That's why we rap them. It makes them nice clean jumpers who never graze the poles."

Natasha, who had been listening to Ginty's explanation, was compelled to stick her oar in. "Rapping is what the professional riders do," she told Issie with a know-it-all tone. "All the showjumping stables do it."

"Come on, Issie." Ginty seemed so self-assured that Issie felt silly for making a fuss and being unprofessional. "You've got half a dozen horses to ride today, so let's get moving!"

Issie's heart was racing as she rode Tokyo to the other end of the arena. Had Natasha been telling the truth when she said all the proper showjumping stables did this? It seemed so cruel to hit the horses in the legs on purpose, but Issie had to have faith in Ginty. She was one of the best trainers in the business. She must know what she was doing.

Beneath her, Tokyo was trotting with a loose, free stride. Issie already instinctively liked the big Hanoverian mare. She seemed sound and sensible. Hopefully, she was a good jumper too – because Issie was about to take her over the upright rail.

As she turned Tokyo to face the rail Issie felt her heart race a little more, but then it always did that when she was about to take a jump. She looked at the fence ahead of her and focused on the task at hand. Tokyo had a huge stride, but she collected up neatly and came in towards the jump with a bouncy canter. Issie pressed her on and counted the canter strides in her head, one, two... three!

They were right in front of the fence when Issie tapped the mare with her heels and Tokyo took off into the air, picking her front feet up and beginning her arc over the jump. If Penny and Verity hadn't lifted the rail, Tokyo would have cleared the fence easily. Instead, Issie felt the jolt, as the mare's legs struck the timber.

Tokyo hadn't been expecting to hit the rail and the shock made her spook and lurch forward when she landed on the other side of the jump. Issie tried to stay with her, but she got left behind as Tokyo charged ahead, and she had to fight to get her seat back. Issie had lost her grip on the reins and by the time she had regained control and pulled the big bay up, they were both rattled and tense.

Ginty, however, didn't seem to notice. "Take her through again," she said. "Let's see if she picks her feet up more this time."

As Issie rode a circle around the jump and gathered Tokyo up to take the fence again, she felt a tight knot of nerves in her tummy. It was a horrible feeling to take your horse towards a fence when you knew the poor thing was going to get whacked in the legs for its trouble!

As they took off Issie found herself almost trying to lift Tokyo over the fence, willing the mare to lift her legs high enough to avoid the blow. But it was no good. Penny and Verity lifted the pole even higher this time and Tokyo's legs smacked hard once more against the raised rail.

"Take her around again!" Ginty called out. "And use the whip this time."

Use the whip. Issie felt herself tense up even more as

Ginty said this. She never used a whip on any of her horses, and she didn't care what Ginty said, she wasn't going to start now. Tokyo wasn't doing anything wrong – she didn't deserve to be hit by a whip as well as the rail! Besides, mares were prone to losing their cool and panicking if they felt confused and Issie could tell that Tokyo was definitely getting anxious as she rode the horse in to the fence once more. Surely the whip would only make it worse?

Coming into the jump this time Tokyo hesitated, and Issie had to put her legs on more strongly to keep her going forward.

"Use your whip! Use your whip!" Ginty ordered loudly. The shouts made Issie panic that Tokyo was going to refuse. She felt compelled to do as the trainer demanded and so, ignoring her own instincts she raised the riding crop and gave Tokyo a thwack. The bay mare surged forward with fright as the blow struck, putting in a short stride before leaping like a startled fawn. It was an ungainly and ugly jump, but she went high in the air, clearing the fence with a huge bound. This time, there was no sound. Tokyo had cleared the raised rail with almost half a metre to spare.

"There!" Ginty said brightly. "You see? It didn't take long for her to learn the lesson, did it?"

Issie knew the jump hadn't been stylish or pleasant, and she felt awful about using the whip. But she had to admit that Ginty had got the result she was after. Tokyo had put extra air between herself and the rail. After that, the girls spent the next half hour schooling the horses over the jumps, and if Tokyo ever looked like she was dropping her hind legs, Verity and Penny would rap her again. By the end of the session the mare was leaping like a gazelle, always clearing the jump with at least twenty centimetres to spare.

"Make sure you ice Tokyo's legs when you put her back in her loose box," Ginty told Issie as she left the arena. "Verity will show you how to use the iceboots."

The iceboots were made out of wetsuit fabric, with pockets fitted to the inside for the ice cubes. Verity showed Issie how to fill them with ice from the freezer, making sure to spread the ice evenly all the way down the boot before she wrapped the first one around Tokyo's left front leg and Velcroed it firmly on.

"What do they need these for?" Issie asked.

"They stop any bruising or swelling from contacting the poles," Verity said.

"Why don't we just bandage their legs beforehand to protect them?" Issie asked.

"We need the horses to feel pain when they hit a jump. It has to hurt them so they learn their lesson – that's how rapping works," Verity replied.

The head groom didn't seem to notice the look of abject horror on Issie's face. She was busy bending back down again to adjust the fastenings on the iceboot.

"Can you fill the next boot with ice and pass it to me?"

Verity clearly didn't want to discuss the virtues of rapping with the new junior groom. But Issie had other matters that she wanted to talk to Verity about, anyway.

"Verity?" Issie asked nervously.

"Uh-huh."

"What were you doing when I saw you earlier in the stall with Tottie?"

Verity glared up at Issie. Her eyes were black and threatening.

"Don't talk about it! Not here!" she hissed under her breath. "I told you, didn't I? If you know what's good for you, then you won't get involved!" Verity stood up and looked nervously around the stall. "You can put the other boot on by yourself," she said flatly. "Leave them on her for twenty minutes then take them off again. I've got to go and get Tottie ready. Meet us back in the arena when you're done. You'll be helping Ginty on the ground this time."

As Issie took up her position opposite Penny, she felt sick to her stomach. It was bad enough being the one jumping over the rail, but lifting it and hitting the horses on purpose felt even worse.

"I don't want to do this," she told Ginty.

The flame-haired trainer seemed genuinely shocked. "Why?"

"Because I'm going to hurt the horses."

Ginty shook her head. "It's for their own good. In the old days people used to let children touch a hotplate on the cooker. They'd burn their fingers, but they would learn the lesson – and they'd never touch the hotplate again. You're the mother trying to teach your child a lesson. If your horse learns to keep their feet up when they jump, isn't that a good thing?"

Issie still didn't really understand. What kind of awful mum would let a kid stick their finger on a hotplate? But she could see that Ginty was fed up with her making a fuss about things. And so Issie reluctantly took up her position next to the jump and stood there with her heart hammering in her chest as Verity rode into the ring on Tottie.

Tottie was a gorgeous mare, with a really swingy trot and lovely dark grey dapples. Issie might not exactly have been a member of the Verity fan club, but she had to admit that Dulmoth Park's head groom rode her really beautifully. Everything about Verity was precise and exact. She always had her body in the perfect position, her hands steady, her eyes up and her heels down.

"How does she feel, Verity?" Ginty asked.

"She's tracking up," Verity replied. "She seems fine."

Issie noticed that Ginty was looking closely at Tottie's hind legs.

"Is there something wrong with her?" Issie asked.

Ginty stayed focused on the mare. "Just making sure that she's level in the back," she told Issie.

Level in the back? Issie thought. That meant Ginty was watching Tottie's back legs to see whether the mare was lame or sore.

Whatever Tottie's problem might have been, Ginty seemed satisfied that there was nothing wrong. "She looks good to me. Bring her over the fence, please."

Verity brought Tottie in towards the fence. Issie stood by, holding the rail, waiting. She was so nervous, her hands were wet with sweat, and she worried that she wouldn't be able to keep her grip on the painted pole.

As the grey mare took off, Issie grasped the rail with both hands and looked across at Penny, waiting for her to give the cue. "OK…" Penny nodded, "do it now!"

The two girls picked up at exactly the same time, hoisting the rail out of its cups and holding it aloft so that Tottie couldn't help but hammer her hind legs against it in mid-air.

Even though Issie knew the blow was coming, she still got a shock as she felt the horse's hind legs connect. The impact reverberated through her own body as she gripped on to the rail, absorbing the blow before lowering the rail back down again and resting it back in the cups.

"Good stuff, girls!" Ginty said, looking pleased.

"Come through again, Verity," she instructed. "And pick up the contact this time!"

Tottie was slower to get the message than Tokyo had been. It took several 'raps' before the mare really began to lift up her feet above the rail.

Issie hated hurting Tottie. Each time the poor mare bashed her legs it made Issie feel sick. But no one else seemed bothered. Penny appeared to be quite relaxed about raising the pole. The two girls must have hoisted it up about a dozen times until finally Tottie lifted her legs high enough and cleared the top rail with lots of space to spare.

"See?" Ginty told Issie. "They all learn in the end."

It was Natasha's turn back in the arena now. The next horse on her roster was Flame, and Issie noticed that the handsome chestnut horse seemed quite anxious. He skipped about, cantering on the spot as Natasha tried to hold him.

"He loves jumping! He's dying to take the fences!" Natasha said as she held the reins taut and tried to calm him down. But Flame wouldn't settle. He kept jogging about, fighting for his head all the way to the other end of the arena until Natasha finally turned him to face the jump.

As soon as Flame had the fence in his sights, the gelding became completely frantic, battling against Natasha, trying to break loose.

Issie could see sweat forming a white froth where the reins were rubbing on the gelding's neck, and he held his head up above the bit. His tail was swishing anxiously and his ears were back. Natasha, meanwhile, was gripping the reins even tighter, as if she were afraid to let the big chestnut loose.

"Hurry up," Ginty told her. "Take him over it, Natasha, and let's see how he goes."

As she said this, Natasha loosened the reins just a smidgen. It was enough for Flame. He shot forward like a cannonball, bearing down on the fence in a full gallop. Issie and Penny didn't raise the rail. Flame was galloping so hard, he couldn't possibly get enough height to clear the fence. Instead, he almost ran through the jump, taking the top two rails with him, and scattering them in his wake.

"Well, that was a disaster!" Ginty said grumpily. "Natasha – you need to collect him up. He can't jump if he's galloping. He's too flat."

"I'm trying to!" Natasha spat back. She was still wrestling with Flame, trying to regain control of the big chestnut. She had managed to get him back to a canter, but Flame was bouncing around beneath her like popcorn in a pot. It was clear that he was ready to explode again.

The next time Natasha pointed Flame at the fence and let him loose, Issie could hardly bear to even watch. If anything it was worse than before. This time, his gallop was so crazy that Penny and Issie actually both found themselves moving away from the sides of the jump in case there was a crash. This was just as well because Flame literally ran through the rails, barely bothering to jump at all, bashing all five poles with his chest and scattering them over the ground.

"Ohmygod!" Issie hurried forward with Penny to pick up the rails and rebuild the jump again. "Is he always like this?"

Penny nodded. "He's getting worse! Ginty has been training him for a couple of weeks since he arrived at the stables. He's really nuts. I don't care how good his bloodlines are. He's bonkers, if you ask me."

All this time, Natasha had been looking more and more nervous about controlling Flame. On the last jump, when Flame had bashed down all the rails, she had barely managed to stay on. Now, as Ginty asked her to bring the imposing chestnut around again, she was clearly terrified. Her face was as white as a sheet.

As Flame danced and crab-stepped in front of them, Natasha turned him towards the fence and this time, to mask her own fear, she gave him several hefty whacks with the whip before she let him go. The result was that Flame shot forward faster than ever before, storming the fence at a mad gallop. Natasha let out a shriek, realising he would never make the jump, and pulled him off to the side so that Issie had to dive out of the way as they galloped past. It took Natasha the full length of the arena to pull the chestnut to a stop and by that time Flame was shaking and dripping with sweat.

"I think that will do for him today, Natasha," Ginty said coolly. "You can take him back to the stables."

Natasha nodded gratefully then turned the chestnut gelding away, riding him back towards the stalls. Issie watched them go, shaking her head in disbelief as Flame continued to side-step, stomp and fret all the way out of the arena.

What a shame, Issie thought. Flame was such a beautiful horse, with such fantastic breeding. But what good was breeding when the horse went totally insane every time he faced a jump?

Issie had to admit that she had been jealous of Natasha scoring the ride on Flame, but that was before she'd seen him going berserk in the arena! He was the clearly the last horse in the stable that anyone would want to ride. Now she was glad that it was Natasha and not her that had been given the ride on the big chestnut. Compared to Flame, Tokyo was a well-schooled dream. The mare was one of the most scopey jumpers she'd ever ridden. She was going to be brilliant in the showjumping ring. It seemed like Issie had lucked out and got the best horse in the stables. She should have known that it was too good to last.

Chapter 5

Issie was horrified when she arrived at work the next morning to find that the blackboard roster had been rewritten, with Natasha down to ride Tokyo! Her eyes widened even more when she scanned down her list of horses for the day. Flame was now written down underneath Issie's name! What was going on?

After grooming Flame, Issie confronted Verity about the changes to the roster, but the head groom wasn't sympathetic. "Ginty asked me to reassign some of the rides," she shrugged. "She told me to give Tokyo to Natasha."

Issie was confused. "Is it because I did something wrong with Tokyo?"

Verity sighed. "How should I know? You'll have to ask Ginty about that."

Issie found Ginty in her office, looking over her paperwork. The trainer seemed surprised at the early-morning interruption.

"What's up?" she asked Issie, without raising her eyes from the neat stack of papers in front of her.

"I… I didn't realise you were unhappy with the way I was riding Tokyo," Issie managed to mumble.

"I'm not," Ginty said. "Actually, you seem surprisingly capable as a rider. I'd expected a lot less from someone who's only had Tom Avery as an instructor."

Issie wasn't really sure what to say. Was that a compliment or an insult? "So why are you taking her off me? Did I do something wrong?"

Ginty shook her head. "Not at all. But Tokyo is an easy horse to handle, which is why I've given the ride to Natasha. She was clearly out of her depth yesterday. You'll take over on Flame. He needs a more capable rider."

Even though she wasn't exactly thrilled that Ginty had swapped her on to Flame, Issie had to admit that she was flattered. Ginty obviously thought that Issie could do a better job than Natasha had done.

"Verity will help you tack him up," Ginty told her. Issie wanted to say that she was perfectly capable of putting a saddle and a bridle on a horse by herself, but she didn't argue. Instead, she headed back to the tack room, where she found Verity holding up a complicated arrangement of steel and leather that Issie had never seen before.

"Have you ever ridden in a Dutch gag?" Verity asked.

The Dutch gag looked like an instrument of torture. Instead of one simple ring at each side of the bridle where the reins attached, the gag bit had four rings and a leather loop.

"They're used for horses that pull or try to bolt," Verity explained. "Flame won't be able to gallop off at the jumps when he's wearing one of these."

"He wasn't wearing this yesterday," Issie said. "Natasha was riding him in an eggbutt snaffle."

"Ginty thought we should swap him to a gag," Verity said. "She thinks 'serious hardware' is what Flame needs."

Issie looked warily at the gag. "Will it hurt him?"

"It's a very common bit," Verity said. "Jumping horses often wear them." Issie noticed that Verity hadn't actually answered her question.

"Come on," Verity said. "I'll show you how to fit it on him. You have to make sure the noseband is tight enough."

The big chestnut gelding was shining like burnished copper. He had good stable manners too. He stood quietly and patiently while Issie fiddled with the straps on his new bridle.

"Are you going to be a good boy for me today in the arena?" Issie whispered to him as she did up the noseband. Flame snuffled her hand softly and nickered back to her in reply and Issie's heart went out to him. OK, Flame had gone crazy yesterday when Natasha was riding him. But perhaps it wasn't Flame who was the problem? After all, Natasha did have a reputation for ruining perfectly good horses. Could it have been Natasha's fault that Flame kept galloping at the jumps? Maybe things would be different now that Issie was riding him.

Despite looking complicated, the Dutch gag wasn't that tricky to put on. Verity helped with the saddle too and then she gave Issie a leg up and tightened the girth up another hole.

"OK," she said. "Take him into the arena and let's see if he goes any better today."

Yesterday Natasha had held Flame permanently on a tight, tight rein to stop him from bolting. Today Issie used a loose rein and the big chestnut seemed perfectly relaxed as she allowed him to stretch his neck as they walked around to warm up. Maybe it was because Issie knew that the Dutch gag bit would give her the power to stop him, but she never worried about the big Hanoverian getting away on her.

"He's looking much better today," Ginty called out to Issie. "Try collecting him up a little on to a shorter rein and get him moving! Let's see how he goes for you."

Issie did as Ginty asked. As she shortened the reins she felt Flame tense up, so she kept talking, trying to calm him with her voice.

When she felt like the horse was walking forward without a fuss, Issie put her legs on and Flame lifted up immediately into the most spectacular trot. He had amazing floaty, Hanoverian paces, which swept along in huge, extended strides that were so enormous they were almost scary to ride. Issie tried his canter and it was even bigger and bolder than the trot! Flame moved so quickly and with such vigour that she had to fight her instinct to grip at the reins and hold him back.

This must have been where Natasha had gone wrong, Issie thought. If you held Flame back because you were afraid of his power, then he would only fight you. You needed to steel your nerve and go with the horse, rather than trying to hold him back.

At least that was what Issie thought, but Ginty seemed to disagree.

"What are you doing?" Ginty demanded. "Hold him back! He's rushing. Restrain him and keep the reins tight. Slow him down as you take him up to the jump!"

The upright rail was still set up in the middle of the arena. Issie did as Ginty said and held Flame tightly in check as they cantered around the corner to face it. The moment the chestnut gelding caught sight of the jump he surged beneath her. Issie wanted to relax and let go, but Ginty had other ideas.

"Bring him back harder!" Ginty insisted. "Use the gag! Make him submit!"

The chestnut was beginning to bob up and down like a jack-in-the-box, just as he had with Natasha. He was crab-stepping again, his body was quivering with tension. His head was way up in the air as he tried to get above the bit, but the gag held him firm. He couldn't gallop off.

"Tight rein! Tight rein! Tighter!" Ginty's cries filled Issie's ears. She did as she was told, hanging off the horse's face until she was a couple of strides out from the jump, when Ginty suddenly yelled, "Let him go now!"

Thrilled to finally be let loose, Flame leapt away from Issie's hands, put in two huge strides and flew the fence with ease. As he landed on the other side of the fence the chestnut fought to stay free of the gag and Issie had to canter a lap of the arena to bring him back under control. It hadn't been the most comfortable jump, but at least he'd gone over. Issie gave Flame a slappy pat on his neck. "Well done, boy!"

"Bring him around and let's do that again," Ginty said brightly.

Issie took Flame over the upright another half a dozen times with Ginty calling out instructions. She was beginning to understand what the trainer wanted from her. Ginty liked it when her riders really held the horse back, keeping the pressure on until the last minute. It was about creating energy so the horses would jump big.

A bit like shaking a fizzy drink and then opening the lid right in front of the jump.

It was a very different style of riding from anything she had learnt with Avery. But in some ways, Issie thought, the two instructors were alike. After all, Avery and Ginty were both focused on getting the best out of their horses. OK, so Ginty's methods were the opposite of Tom's, but that didn't mean they were wrong. Issie had to trust Ginty and do what she said – then she would get results.

The gag was definitely helping Issie to hold Flame as she worked him around the arena. Once Ginty was satisfied with the way Flame took the upright rail, she asked Issie to ride him over some of the other jumps. There was a treble, a small oxer and a little brick wall. Issie took him around the three fences one at a time before Ginty told her that was enough for today and she could put him back in the stables.

"He's performing very nicely with the new bit," Ginty told her. "Ride him in the gag from now on."

Ginty set a fast pace for her riders at Dulmoth Park. When you were riding six horses in one day there wasn't time to stand around and analyse your performance afterwards. Issie only had a few minutes to wash down Flame, run the sweat scraper over him and rug him up again, before she was busy saddling up her next mount.

Her next pony on the roster that morning was Orlando, a fourteen-two fleabitten grey with a Roman nose. It didn't take Issie long to saddle him up, and by the time she was back in the arena, Verity was about to bring Tottie in as well.

As Verity worked the dapple-grey mare around the edge of the arena, Issie could see that something was wrong. Tottie's strides were uneven and the mare looked miserable. She was swishing her tail and her ears were flat back – signs that a horse is unhappy or in pain. Even at a quick glance it was clear to see that poor Tottie was lame on one of her hind legs.

Ginty shook her head with disappointment. "Put Tottie back in the stables, Verity, she's favouring that left leg." And that was it. The grey mare's workout was over before it had begun.

It was a busy morning at the stables. Issie rode four horses before lunch and then the girls were kept busy cleaning tack and mucking out the stalls. The farrier was due that afternoon too, and Ginty asked Issie if she would mind staying back after four to help her deal with the horses needing to be shod.

It was five thirty when the farrier finally finished the last horse. Issie had tidied up the tack room and was just about to get her bike and cycle home when she noticed that someone was still riding in the arena.

It was Verity. The head groom was mounted up on Tottie once again, despite the fact that Ginty had told her quite clearly that the mare was lame and shouldn't be ridden.

Issie watched as Verity began to trot Tottie around the arena. Something very strange was going on. Issie found herself staring almost hypnotically at the mare's hind legs as she trotted in serpentines between the fences. Issie couldn't believe it. *Tottie had definitely been lame that morning.* She had seen it with her own eyes. But now the mare was trotting perfectly. She wasn't lame at all! It was impossible. Tottie was cured.

Chapter 6

After spending her first week at Dulmoth Park, doing twelve-hour shifts, riding six horses each day, grooming them, mucking out stalls and doing all the hard feeds, Issie didn't really feel like riding her own ponies. But she had promised Kate and Stella that she would go hacking on Sunday, so she cycled to the River Paddock that afternoon to meet them, her legs aching as she pedalled.

Stella and Kate were already waiting at the gate with Marmite and Toby tacked up, dying to hear all the details. "So how was it?" Stella asked eagerly.

"Two words," Issie said as she parked her bike beside the others. "Natasha. Tucker."

Stella couldn't believe it when Issie told her that

Natasha was the other new groom at Ginty's stables. "Ohmygod! Stuck-up Tucker must be so furious that she's working with you!"

"Well, I'm not exactly thrilled about it either," Issie groaned. "It's even worse now since Ginty made us swap horses. I'm sure Natasha thinks I suggested the swap – she hasn't spoken to me since – even though she got the better deal, if you ask me!"

"I think I'd rather be stacking supermarket shelves after all!" Stella said.

"Wait," Issie told her, "there's more, and it gets worse." And she filled them in on the dramas at Dulmoth Park, including Verity's strange behaviour and Tottie's curious come-and-go lameness.

"How can a horse be totally sore in the morning and fine again in the afternoon?" Stella said. "That just doesn't happen!"

"The farrier had been," Kate said. "Perhaps she had something wrong with one of her shoes and he fixed it?"

Issie shook her head. "The farrier didn't shoe Tottie – he didn't even go near her. He was only replacing the shoes on Baxter, Quebec and Tanga."

"What about that injection Verity gave her?" Kate asked. "What do you think was in that?"

"I don't know," Issie sighed. "Maybe it was vitamins or something? It's a professional stable and they feed them all these supplements. They do things differently there."

"I still think you should go and talk to Avery about it," Kate insisted. "You should tell him about the rapping too. Making horses hit jumps on purpose sounds weird to me."

Issie shook her head. "I can't. Tom already loathes Ginty. He'll just say 'I told you so'. Besides, I can't go behind Ginty's back and complain about her to another trainer. Her methods are different, but they must work, because she's really well-respected." Issie paused. "I don't think I'm explaining the rapping very well. It sounds awful, but it wasn't that bad. By the end of the lesson Tokyo and the other horses were all clearing the jump by miles."

Kate looked doubtful. "I still think it's hideous."

"You didn't see it!" Issie insisted. "It actually seemed to work, and the horses were OK..."

As they hacked their horses out together that evening, it felt so nice to be back with Stella and Kate, laughing about Stuck-up Tucker and gossiping about the goings-on at pony club. Still, at times Issie felt kind of distant from her friends. She had missed out on yesterday's pony-club rally because she had to work. And she wouldn't be going to the rally next weekend either. She'd be riding in her first proper event as part of the Dulmoth Park team. They would be heading south to the Sandilands showgrounds to compete at the first showjumping fixture of the season.

That's what Stella and Kate don't understand, Issie thought. She was riding as a professional now, and they weren't. They didn't have the right to judge Ginty's methods. If they had been there then they would have seen how effective the rapping technique had been. Didn't they realise that Ginty had been at the top of the showjumping circuit for years? This was a proper stable, not a pony club. It was a totally different world. And it was one that Issie was excited to be part of.

Ginty's horse truck could only fit seven horses, and since there were over twenty horses in the stables it was going to be a tough call deciding who to take to the show. For the next week, Ginty assessed the progress of the horses and figured out which ones would be going to Sandilands.

"It's got to be a mix of advanced horses and the new, young stock needing some experience," Verity explained to Issie as she chalked up Ginty's chosen list on the board in the tack room. "Not all of the horses in this stable are destined for greatness. Some of them will never amount to much, but if we can take them out and give them some showring experience and even win a few ribbons then they'll be worth much more money when they are sold."

Despite his ongoing problems with rushing the fences, Ginty had decided that Flame needed the competition experience and would be travelling to Sandilands.

"He's young and green and he needs the outing," Verity said. "He'll be jumping in a couple of minor classes – not big fences."

Tottie was also on the list. Issie had kept an eye on the mare ever since she had seen Verity riding her the previous week and she seemed to be quite sound. After jumping her on Wednesday, Verity had taken her on a road ride on the Thursday, even trotting on the tarmac. By the time the chalkboard list was written up on the Friday, Ginty seemed to have no qualms about taking Tottie with them to Sandilands.

Issie's other ride at Sandilands would be Quebec, a sweet-natured dun pony that she had been riding regularly for the past two weeks, who was a very clever jumper. Natasha was riding Tokyo and a green young pony named Baxter, and Penny was down to ride Sebastian and Vertigo.

That night, before she went home, Ginty called the girls together and gave Issie and Natasha a purple Dulmoth Park sweatshirt each, just like the ones Penny and Verity wore. "You're part of the team," she told them. "You have to look the part."

"Big day tomorrow then!" Mrs Brown said as she dished up the fish pie for dinner that evening. "Are you excited?"

"I'm too nervous to eat!" Issie said. It was always a

bit funny the night before a competition, but this was worse than usual.

"The owner is going to be there tomorrow watching us," Issie told her mum. As she said this she felt something damp pressing into her hand. Wombat, who had been curled up at Issie's feet under the table, had stuck his snout in her lap and was nudging her with his moist nose. He usually sat in this position at mealtimes in the hope that Issie would smuggle him titbits from her plate. But it was hard to smuggle pieces of sloppy fish pie under the table, so tonight he was out of luck.

Mrs Brown was confused. "I thought Ginty was the owner?"

Issie had to explain to her mum how Cassandra Steele actually owned most of the horses at Dulmoth Park.

"She owns the two horses that I'll be riding tomorrow – Flame and Quebec," Issie said.

"So is this a big show?" Mrs Brown wanted to know. "Is that why the owner's coming to watch? Do you want me to come along too?"

Issie shrugged. "You don't have to. It's an hour's drive and it's not a big event. Lots of the big-name riders will be there, though, because the competition points count towards the accumulator for the Horse of the Year. The big show is the North Island champs at the end of next month."

"Are Stella and Kate going to this show tomorrow?" Mrs Brown asked.

Issie shook her head. "They've got pony club."

Mrs Brown reached across the table and forked a serving of salad on to her plate. "What about Tom?"

"He'll be at pony club too," Issie said. She was assuming this. She didn't actually know for certain, because she hadn't spoken to him since they'd had the fight about her going to work for Ginty.

"Well," Mrs Brown said with a mischievous grin, "I suppose you'll be hanging out with Natasha then."

Issie groaned. "Thanks for that, Mum."

Mrs Brown obviously thought it was funny that Issie had ended up being stuck with Natasha for the holidays. She had no idea just how bad things had got between the girls over the past fortnight. It was crazy – Issie should have been the one holding the grudge, since she'd had to give up the ride on Tokyo. But Natasha was still angry with Issie over the trouble she'd caused her father. Issie had exposed Mr Tucker's underhand plans to build luxury apartments next door to the golf club by taking over the lease on Chevalier Point Pony Club land. Thankfully his dodgy business deal had been thwarted. But it was an expensive blow for the property developer, and Natasha clearly blamed Issie for her father's ongoing money worries.

Issie had steered clear of Stuck-up Tucker as much as she could. The two girls were on speaking terms, but only just. Natasha could barely bring herself to grunt hello most mornings.

At the stables it wasn't a big deal because they were so busy working and riding the whole time. But on Saturday, it was a different matter. When Issie turned up at Dulmoth Park to load the horses on to the truck, she discovered that the senior grooms had already organised the seating arrangements. Verity and Penny had put themselves up the front in the cab with Ginty and left Issie in the back alone with Natasha and the horses.

Even with seven horses on board, the truck had loads of room inside. It was like a Tardis – somehow it was bigger on the inside than it looked from the outside. The horse stalls were totally space-age, with heavily padded barriers and rubber matting. The rider's area was plush too, with suede banquette seating that folded out into bunk beds for overnight trips, and a rather chic kitchen with a marble benchtop and a dining table. Issie and Natasha both took up positions on either end of one of the suede banquettes, with the dogs – Wombat, Jock and Angus – forming a canine barricade between them, as Ginty pulled the truck out on to the main road and headed for Sandilands.

The journey was one of the longest hours of Issie's life. Natasha spent most of the time pointedly ignoring Issie and texting on her hot-pink mobile phone, reading back the messages to herself and giggling as if they were hysterically funny. After about half an hour of this, however, she seemed to get bored with her texts and turned to Issie instead.

"It's pony club today, isn't it?" she asked, already knowing the answer to her own question. "I'm surprised Avery has let you take the day off to go showjumping."

"I didn't tell him…" Issie began and instantly regretted it. She didn't want to talk to Natasha about this.

"What?" Natasha's ears pricked up. "He doesn't know

you're not going to be at his little rally? Or he doesn't know that you're going showjumping with us?"

"Both," Issie said.

"Well, I can't imagine he'll be very pleased when he finds out," Natasha said smugly. "His star pupil abandoning him like that."

"I'm not," Issie said. "I mean, I don't have a choice. This is my job."

"Yeah, right. Like you didn't have a choice about ruining my father's property development," Natasha shot back.

In a way, Issie had been waiting for Natasha to bring this up. She knew that the bratty blonde had been festering over this ever since the Golden Trophy.

"Verity told me that you have to work at Ginty's because of your dad's money problems," Issie began.

"My dad wouldn't have money problems if it wasn't for you!" Natasha's eyes went red and it looked like she was going to cry. "He'd be furious if he knew I was even speaking to you. And Verity shouldn't be talking about my family's business to anyone either!"

"She wasn't gossiping," Issie insisted. "Honestly, Natasha. I'm really sorry about what happened to your dad. I know you must hate having to work with me. But as long as we're stuck together, we might as well try and get along. I'd like to try and be friends."

It was a heartfelt plea, but it seemed like it fell on deaf ears. Natasha ignored her and went back to sending texts once more. Issie sighed. At least she'd tried.

There was silence in the truck for a while longer and then Natasha giggled again at another text. This time, though, she handed the phone over to Issie. There, on the screen, was a joke.

Q: What do you call a horse who lives next door?
A: A neigh-bour!

Issie laughed. "That's so cheesy!"

Natasha gave a slight smile. "There are some other ones I've been sent that are much funnier – here, I'll show you…"

By the time Ginty pulled up at the showgrounds twenty minutes later, there had been a distinct thawing in relations between Issie and Natasha. It wasn't like they were suddenly besties, but at least they were now on speaking terms. Natasha even helped to untie Quebec and led him down the ramp while Issie managed Tokyo and Flame.

The girls tied the horses up to the side of the truck and then Issie ran back up the ramp to help Verity and Penny organise the grooming kit.

"It's pretty here, isn't it? They're really lovely grounds," Issie said, looking out over the green fields of Sandilands to the bush-clad hills that surrounded the arenas.

"Yeah, real scenic," Verity said sarcastically. "Remind me to get it listed as an area of natural beauty. Can you hurry up and finish undoing their floating boots? I need you to go and get some water too, Tottie's managed to get poo all through her tail."

Issie quickly realised that travelling with the Dulmoth Park team wasn't like going away to a show with Stella and Kate. Penny and Verity had been on the road for so many seasons they seemed bored by the whole showjumping business. Ginty, meanwhile, had completely disappeared as soon as she parked the truck.

"She's gone to meet Cassandra," Verity said. "We'd better have everything ready by the time they come back." She turned to Issie and handed her a bucket. "Can you go find a tap and fill this? Then get some

Manes 'n' Tails shampoo out of the kit and wash that dung out of Tottie's tail."

Wombat, Jock and Angus bounded along together beside Issie on the walk to the water tap. Since Issie had started taking Wombat with her to work each day the three dogs had become firm friends. Even though Wombat was the biggest by far, little Jock was clearly the leader of the pack, and he was the one that stuck closest to Issie as they stood in the queue waiting for their turn at the tap. It seemed like everyone else at Sandilands needed water that morning too. There was a huge queue and only one water faucet! Issie had to wait her turn as the riders in front of her put their buckets underneath the nozzle and waited for the steady trickle to fill up their containers. The tap was really slow and it seemed to be taking forever.

Issie had finally reached the front of the line when another rider suddenly swooped in, jumping the queue ahead of Issie, with two really big buckets. After waiting patiently for so long, this was the final straw.

"Hey!" Issie said, reaching out and tapping the other rider on the shoulder. "Hey, you! You're pushing in. It's my turn!"

"I tell you what," the boy responded without turning round, "I'll let you go ahead of me if you give me a kiss."

Issie was flabbergasted! Did he really just say that?

"Wow. I finally managed to say something that shut you up for once!" The boy laughed as he turned round to face her. He had jet-black hair with a long fringe that he casually pushed back off his face to reveal startling pale blue eyes.

"Hello, Issie," he said softly, "I didn't expect to see you here."

Issie found herself suddenly unable to breathe. She couldn't believe it. It was Aidan.

Chapter 7

It had been nearly four months since Issie had broken up with Aidan, but she still often found herself thinking about him, wondering how he was and what he was doing.

She had first met the dark-haired boy with magnetic blue eyes two summers ago at her Aunt Hester's Blackthorn Farm in Gisborne. Aidan worked for Hester as her stable manager. He and Issie had become good friends straight away, but it wasn't until the next summer, when she went back to help Hester with the riding school at the farm, that they finally got together. She remembered how romantic it was the day he kissed her in front of everyone on the lawn underneath the cherry tree.

In the end, their relationship had proved impossible – with Aidan living and working at the farm and Issie a six-hour drive away at Chevalier Point, they never saw each other and Issie decided it was fairer on both of them if she ended it. She had regrets about her decision even then, and now as she looked at Aidan, so handsome in his crisp white jodhpurs and pale blue shirt, she found it hard to imagine how she could ever have broken up with him.

"What... what are you doing here?" Issie finally managed to get a sentence out.

Aidan grinned. "The same as you, I guess – riding."

"Is Aunty Hess here too?"

Aidan shook his head. "She's back at the farm. She's completely wrapped up in training. She needs to get Diablo and Titan ready for a new movie that starts filming in a couple of weeks."

Hester ran a company called the Daredevil Ponies and her movie stunt horses were renowned as the best in the business.

"So why aren't you with Aunty Hess?"

"She doesn't need me until filming begins. She can handle training Diablo and Titan on her own. Besides, we sold two more young Blackthorn Ponies to Araminta recently, and Hester thought it would be good if I stayed with the horses to settle them in. I'm going to be working with Araminta at her stables for a couple of weeks," Aidan explained.

Blackthorn Ponies were a wild breed that roamed the hills around Gisborne. They weren't big horses – most of them averaged about fourteen hands – but they were excellent jumpers. In fact they were so good that Hester, Issie and Aidan had gone into business together, schooling Blackthorn Ponies to be sold as showjumpers. Several Blackthorns had been schooled up by Aidan and Issie and were already being ridden competitively on the showjumping circuit.

Issie's own pony, Comet, was a Blackthorn, and Araminta Chatswood-Smith had several of them in her substantial stable of showjumpers – including the piebald pony, Fortune. It was Issie who had been responsible for Fortune's schooling and she'd been looking forward to seeing him again on the showjumping circuit. However, she hadn't expected to see Aidan too.

Aidan took Issie's empty bucket and began to fill it up for her.

"This is so typical of you!" Issie said. She found herself getting flustered. Having Aidan turn up out of the blue had totally thrown her. "Why didn't you tell me you were going to be here?"

"First of all," Aidan said, smiling sweetly back at her as he passed her back the bucket, "we broke up, remember? I don't have to tell you everything any more. Second, I didn't know you were going to be here either. Shouldn't you be at pony club?"

"I'm here for work," Issie found herself hesitating. "I'm… I'm riding for Ginty McLintoch."

"Riding for Ginty? You're kidding!"

"Why?" Issie asked defensively. "I don't see why everyone has to react like that. She's not so bad once you know her!" She picked up her water bucket to leave, and Jock, Angus and Wombat, who had been sitting waiting patiently, all sprang up in unison ready to walk by her side.

"Whoa, don't storm off!" Aidan teased. "You'll spill your water and then you'll have to queue all over again."

"I'm not being a drama queen," Issie insisted, "but I really have to go. I need to wash Tottie's tail before Ginty gets back."

"Oh, come on!" Aidan said. "There's still loads of time before the first class. Come back to the truck with me. Just for a minute."

"I can't," Issie resisted, "I've got the dogs with me..."

But Aidan was insistent. "The dogs can come too. Araminta and Morgan would love to say hi. And you have to come and see Fortune. It'll only take a minute..."

"OK," Issie said. "But just for a minute, and then I have to get back to wash Tottie's tail."

"Great!" Aidan grinned. "You can explain to Araminta how come you're now working for The Enemy!" He said this last part with a spooky horror-movie voice and then grinned again. It was that same grin he always used to give Issie when he was teasing her and at that moment she could feel her heart beating like crazy. It was so strange to see Aidan again. He hadn't changed at all. Well, actually, maybe he was a bit more handsome. Ohmygod! Why did he have to be here? She needed to concentrate on her riding today. Ginty and Cassandra Steele would both be watching her. She couldn't afford to lose focus because her boyfriend... no, she corrected herself, her *ex-boyfriend*... had turned up.

Among the other plain, boring horse trucks, Araminta's truck was ultra-glamorous, like a giant jewel box, painted in crisp white with her initials written on the side in gigantic curlicued Tiffany-blue type. The back ramp of the truck had been left open and there was a girl, about Issie's age, with long dark hair just like Issie's, sitting with her legs dangling off the side of the ramp, busily polishing a Mylar bit.

"Issie!" Morgan Chatswood-Smith dropped the bridle and jumped up and raced over to them, giving Issie a hug. "Mum!" she called out. "Come and see who's here!"

Araminta emerged a few moments later. She looked stunning as always in her usual uniform of sleek jodhpurs and a crisp navy blouse. An orange Hermès scarf tied back her raven hair and she wore a pair of enormous black sunglasses.

"Isadora," Araminta smiled at her. "How nice to see you! Is Tom here with you?"

Aidan pulled a face. "Issie's not here with Tom. She's riding for Ginty!"

"Really?" Araminta looked surprised. "How on earth did that happen?"

"It's a long story," Issie groaned.

"Come on," Aidan said, saving her from the conversation by grabbing her hand and dragging her off. "You have to come and see Fortune."

On the other side of Araminta's sparkling white horse truck the ponies were tied up, each one with their own hay net. They were standing quietly, nibbling away on their hay. All except the piebald pony at the end. He had already finished his whole hay net and was lying down in the shade of the truck, sound asleep.

"Fortune!" Issie giggled at the sight of him. "You haven't changed one bit."

"He likes to catnap between events," Araminta said, shaking her head in disbelief. "He is the craziest pony I've ever owned, but by heavens he can jump! He's been doing one metre thirty at home in the arena—"

"Issie?" Natasha suddenly emerged from round the corner of the horse truck. "Ohmygod, I have been looking everywhere for you! Come on! You're supposed to be sorting out Tottie's tail and Verity is on the warpath looking for you! She says Cassandra will be here soon!"

Issie felt a wave of panic. "I better go!" she told Aidan. "I'll see you later, OK?" She didn't even wait for his reply, and grabbed her bucket.

Natasha wanted them to run back to the truck, but Issie couldn't with the heavy water bucket. "I saw Araminta's truck," Natasha explained as she scurried along beside Issie, urging her to walk faster, "and I figured out straight away that was where you'd be! Ginty is going to hit the roof. She won't care that Aidan is your boyfriend. In fact that makes it worse! As far as Ginty is concerned they're the competition. That's like being a traitor!"

"It's not!" Issie laughed. "And Aidan's not my boyfriend any more. We split up months ago."

Then again, the way that Aidan had flirted with her that morning… OK, so he was only joking when he said the stuff about kissing, but it had still left Issie feeling confused. Did Aidan want to go out with her again?

All happy thoughts of Aidan were wiped from her mind when she saw Verity. The head groom was standing beside Tottie, and she looked utterly furious.

"You took long enough!" Verity exclaimed. "Did you have to dig your own well or something?"

"I'm sorry," Issie said, "I ran into an old friend by the—"

"Yeah, yeah, whatever," Verity said, clearly having no interest in hearing the story. She looked really stressed out. "Can you hurry up and clean Tottie's tail, like, now? Ginty's going to be here any moment with Cassandra."

There was barely enough time to shampoo and rinse Tottie's tail. Issie was just combing out the wet, silvery strands, when Ginty and Cassandra arrived back at the truck.

Issie wasn't sure what she had been expecting Cassandra Steele to look like, but this woman with Ginty certainly wasn't it. Cassandra looked like a bulldog in a trouser suit. She wore a high-collared Chanel tweed jacket, which exaggerated her short and buxom physique and pushed up against the fleshy folds of her face. She had a tight-lipped expression and inquisitive eyes.

She looked at Issie, assessing her from head to toe, as if she were inspecting a pony that she was interested in purchasing. Not saying a word to Issie, she simply turned her attention to Tottie and spoke directly to Ginty.

"How's my wonderful girl doing?" she asked in a booming voice that was far too large for her little body.

"Tottenham Hotspur has been doing extremely well in her training," Ginty replied. "Verity is riding her today, and I think you'll be really pleased with her progress. We're expecting big things from this mare."

"So you must be Verity, then?" Cassandra turned now to Issie, who was still combing through Tottie's tail.

"No, I'm Issie." Issie almost felt like she should bow or curtsey or something when Cassandra spoke to her.

"Isadora has just come on board as one of my new junior riders during the school holidays," Ginty explained. "She's got great potential."

"I see," Cassandra said. "And who were you riding for last season, Isadora?"

"Ummm," Issie didn't know what to say. "I was at Chevalier Point Pony Club."

"Really?" Cassandra raised an eyebrow as if she had just bought an apple and discovered there was a worm in it and wanted her money back. "Pony club, you say? Well, this must be a big step up for you. I hope it's not too big." She focused her attention back to Tottie.

"As you can see, we've got her in brilliant condition," Ginty said enthusiastically.

"I should hope so too!" Cassandra said. "That's why I'm paying you so much money, isn't it?"

Issie began to giggle at this and then realised her mistake and immediately shut up. It was clear that Cassandra hadn't intended this to be a joke.

"And how is Quebec?" Cassandra asked, moving on to the dun pony that was tied up beside Tottie.

Quebec was really fourteen-three hands high, too big for the pony classes, but Ginty had somehow managed to get him under the measure and so he had a lifetime certificate that stated he was fourteen hands and two inches. This meant that Quebec could compete in the fourteen-two-and-under classes against ponies, instead of being pitted against enormous hacks. It also meant that Issie, who was only fifteen, quite light and not too tall, was the ideal choice to ride him.

For the past week Issie had been schooling the little dun over fences at Dulmoth Park, getting used to his ways. Quebec was a sweetheart to ride. He never ever hesitated at a jump, and Issie had no concerns about him refusing. She did worry, though, that he could be sloppy with his legs and might knock down a rail or two, especially in a jump-off.

"Quebec should easily win his grade today," Ginty reassured Cassandra. Issie thought that was a bit rash, telling the owner that her horse would definitely win! She felt a sudden attack of nerves. As Quebec's rider the responsibility was on her shoulders. Ginty had just made it clear that nothing less than a first-place ribbon would do!

"And how is the new lad settling in?" Cassandra put a hand out to stroke Flame's nose. "I paid a lot of money to import this boy. I'm expecting big things."

"He won't disappoint you," Ginty said. "He's been training like a champion already."

Issie boggled at this comment. Why didn't Ginty tell Cassandra the truth? Flame became a certifiable lunatic the minute he saw a showjump in front of him!

There was a little bit of small talk after that about farriers and the rising cost of hard feed. All the time Ginty was talking to Cassandra she seemed awfully tense. It was only when Cassandra excused herself briefly to go and make a call on her mobile phone that Issie found out what was eating Ginty. The trainer had clearly been deeply furious with Issie the whole time and it was only now that Cassandra was out of earshot that she rounded on her junior groom.

"What the devil is going on here?" Ginty hissed under her breath, talking quietly enough to ensure that Cassandra wouldn't hear her. "I get back to the truck and Verity tells me that you've been off God-knows-where doing who-knows-what when you should be getting Tottie ready! You only just got the dung out of her tail in time! Are you trying to make me look bad in front of Cassandra?"

Issie didn't know what to say. "I'm sorry. I was over at Araminta's truck. I ran into an old friend and I thought I'd have enough time—"

"Araminta?" Ginty's eyebrows shot up. "We're not here for socialising, especially not at other people's trucks! You are being paid to ride for me, and you should be getting your horses ready. There's an event about to start! Instead, you're off chatting to the competition and leaving it up to your teammates. It's not good enough!"

Ginty looked utterly furious and her voice was as cold as ice. "I expect total loyalty from my riders. I have got rid of grooms for this sort of behaviour before, and I have no qualms about doing it again!" She took a deep breath. "Do you want to keep this job, Isadora? Because right now… I'm on the verge of firing you!"

Chapter 8

Ginty's temper tantrum was vicious, but it proved to be shortlived. She calmed down as soon as Cassandra came back from making her phone call, and it became clear that she had been bluffing about firing Issie.

"It's a hollow threat," Verity sighed. "She's not going to get rid of you – she just told Cassandra how great you are. If she fires you now it will make her look bad."

The four girls were heading towards the arena to walk the course before the competition began. Penny and Natasha had gone ahead, and Issie was walking at the back with Verity. "I'm sorry she gave you such a hard time when I told her that you'd been over at Araminta's truck," Verity continued, "but I did it for your own good. You need to sharpen up and learn how things work around here, Issie. You never, ever leave the horses unattended at an event. Especially when the boss is due to turn up!"

"But I was only going to talk to my friends—"

Verity cut her off. "You don't have friends any more, Issie. This is a serious competition. When you work for Ginty, you aren't even allowed to talk to the other riders."

"Not even to say hello?" Issie couldn't believe it. There were lots of things about Ginty that surprised her. Even what they were doing at this moment seemed wrong. Avery would never have let Issie walk a showjumping course without being there right next to her advising on the best way to take each jump.

"Oh, Ginty hardly ever walks the course with us," Verity said dismissively when Issie asked why the trainer wasn't with them. "She's always too busy schmoozing the other owners and looking for horses to buy. Ginty's worse when Cassandra is here watching," she added. "She's terrified that we'll make her look bad."

"I don't think Cassandra likes me much," Issie said.

"She doesn't like anyone!" Verity said. "She must have met me a half a dozen times and she never even remembers my name. She only cares about the horses."

"Does she ride?" Issie asked.

Verity gave a wry laugh. "Does it look like she rides?" She shook her head. "Cassandra's the head of some big company and she's super-rich. I suppose she needs to spend her money on something so it might as well be horses – even if she gets other people to ride them for her."

"She seems to really love being around the horses," Issie said.

"I know!" Verity sighed. "I wish she'd push off. She makes Ginty all uptight – and besides, I can't get anything done with her nosying around."

Verity got her wish. By the time they returned from walking the course, Cassandra was gone and Ginty was bent over Quebec's front hoof with a tiny wrench in her right hand, screwing studs into the pony's shoes so he wouldn't slip on the grass in the arena.

"How does the course look?" Ginty asked without looking up at them.

"The jumps are at maximum height for the hack

ring," Verity told her. "And the ground is quite hard. Tottie will definitely need studs."

"The pony ring is pretty straightforward," Issie said. "The only jump that might cause trouble is a tight corner into the oxer."

"Quebec is good on tight turns," Ginty reassured her.

While Ginty finished the last of the pony's studs, she sent Verity into the horse truck. "I think Quebec could do with some liniment," Ginty told her. "Can you put it on, please?"

Verity didn't look pleased about this, but she did as Ginty asked. She emerged from the truck wearing a pair of rubber gloves and carrying a tube of creamy paste, which she rubbed quickly into the front of all four of Quebec's legs. The cream dissolved as she rubbed it in so that it couldn't be seen.

"What's that for?" Issie asked.

"It's a therapeutic rub," Ginty said vaguely.

Issie had seen riders use white grease on their horses' legs for eventing, but she'd never seen anyone apply a rub before showjumping. Mind you, she'd never used studs in her pony's shoes either. That was the difference between being a pony-club rider and being a professional, she realised. There were so many tricks of the trade that she knew nothing about.

There were three jumping arenas at Sandilands. Issie would be riding in arena number one, the pony ring, on Quebec. As she warmed the pony up in the practice arena, Issie could feel the nerves forming a tight knot in her tummy. She recognised so many famous faces here today, riders who had been on the showjumping circuit for years, all of them with their strings of perfect, polished jumping ponies. Competing against them, especially with Cassandra Steele watching her, suddenly felt like a big step indeed.

When they called her name, Issie rode into the arena straight away, and did a whole lap around the jumps before the bell rang. The bell signalled that she had one minute left before she had to ride Quebec through the flags to begin their round. She crossed the start line at a fast canter and had the first jump in her sights before she checked the pony hard with the reins, just as Ginty had instructed. She held Quebec until they were just a couple of strides out from the fence before she let him loose again and the little dun bounded forward and flew the fence cleanly. As soon as they were on the other side he tried to charge off with her, but Issie was too quick, gathering him back up again into a tightly controlled canter, just as Ginty had coached her to do in the training sessions.

Issie had thought Ginty was being overly optimistic when she told Cassandra that Quebec would win his class today, but maybe the flame-haired trainer was right. As Quebec flew clear over jump after jump, luck certainly seemed to be on their side. Normally, back in Ginty's yard, riding Quebec tended to be like a giant game of pick-up-sticks because the pony was so prone to knocking down rails. But not today in the show ring. Quebec's hooves never so much as brushed a pole as he took the fences one after the other with ease. Issie rode out of the arena with a huge grin on her face. Clear round!

There was a burst of applause from Cassandra on the sidelines.

"Excellent work!" Ginty beamed at her as Issie came out of the arena. "Good stuff."

"He was so much better than he is at Dulmoth!" Issie enthused.

"Quebec always rides perfectly at home," Ginty corrected her, knowing that Cassandra was standing nearby and could hear them. "But you're right, he was particularly brilliant in there. Some horses like to perform in front of a crowd."

It turned out to be a morning of triumphs. Issie and Quebec had taken first place in the class just as Ginty predicted they would. Verity, meanwhile, had also taken first place in the hack ring on Tottie, who seemed absolutely sound, with not a trace of lameness. Natasha and Tokyo had come third in their class too, while Penny's horse, Vertigo, had done the slightly faster time to come second ahead of them. By the time they stopped for lunch break it was official: the Dulmoth Park team were at the top of the accumulator table!

Being on the winning team can turn even the bitterest enemies into firm friends. The success of Team Ginty was so infectious that Natasha was suddenly acting like she and Issie were besties.

"Even Araminta Chatswood-Smith's team haven't got more points than us," Natasha told Issie, beaming from ear to ear as they tied up the horses and gave them their hay nets. "We totally rule!"

Their reign at the top of the table, though, was about to take a blow. As Issie mounted up on Flame for his first event, she could sense straight away that the horse was tense. And as they warmed up over the practice jump, Flame was pulling like a train.

"Hold him back!" Ginty instructed her as Issie turned Flame to face the practice jump – a low cross-rail. "Hold him all the way. Look for the stride and then release!"

Issie did as Ginty said. At the very last minute, about two strides out from the jump, she let the reins slacken and Flame virtually bolted! He took the fence at a frantic gallop, acting totally strung-out. It took Issie all her strength to pull him up – even with the gag bit. She was worried that Flame was getting out of control. But when she got back to Ginty's side, the trainer seemed unfazed by his mad behaviour.

"He's a bit eager," was Ginty's assessment of the situation. "Just remember to hang on tight until you see your stride," she passed Issie the whip, "and use this."

They were at the gates of the arena now and Flame's

name was being called over the loudspeaker. Even though the jumps in the hack ring for his class were only eighty centimetres – which should have been a breeze for a horse of his size – Issie still felt worried. Flame was crab-stepping now, fighting against her hands and constantly grabbing at the reins as if he might bolt at any moment.

All she could hope was that once they entered the arena, Flame would settle down. It was foolish optimism, of course. If anything, the horse was much worse. He was virtually cantering on the spot and his head was up high above the bit. He wasn't listening to Issie at all! As they set off to begin their round Flame was in a disunited canter as he raced through the flags. The gag bit seemed to be doing nothing whatsoever, and she had to fight him like mad to bring him back in front of the first fence and look to find a stride. Despite her efforts, Flame jumped long, landing badly and taking out half the fence with his hind legs. It was the same over the next jump and the one after that. The poles fell like skittles and every time Flame hit a rail with his legs he seemed almost to leap out of his skin. It was as if his legs were being given electric shocks each time they struck the jumps.

It was the maddest round Issie had ever ridden in her life, and they finished on twenty-eight faults. Issie was just glad they had made it through the course alive. Flame was so strung-out he was dangerous.

This time as she left the arena, Cassandra Steele didn't look so pleased, and neither did Ginty.

"Take him for a cool-down walk," Ginty told her with a sour face. "And then unsaddle him and wash him down. He's supposed to be in one more class today, but after that performance I think we'll withdraw him."

Natasha had finished riding on Tokyo for the day too and was already at the wash bays, about to start hosing the mare down.

"I saw Flame acting up in there," Natasha said, shaking her head. "It's not your fault. That horse is nuts."

Issie didn't know what to say. She waited for her turn in the wash bay, watching as Natasha bent down to undo the bell boots on Tokyo's front legs. Natasha ripped off the boots and then her face suddenly went white as a sheet and she began to squeal in pain.

"Ohmygod! Owww!"

"What is it?" Issie was confused. "What's wrong? Did she stand on your foot or something?"

"No! It's my hand!" Natasha shrieked. "My right hand! It feels like it's on fire!"

"What have you done to it?" Issie asked.

"I haven't done doing anything! I was just taking off her boots," Natasha said, "and I felt something sticky on my hand. Oww! It's burning!"

Issie looked down at Tokyo's legs. They were damp and sticky. "It must be the liniment!" Issie said. "Verity was putting it on the horses before they jumped. I saw her put it on Quebec. She was wearing gloves."

"Get it off me!" Natasha was yelling. Her eyes were wide and her face was white with pain.

"Put the hose on it!" Issie said. There was no one else around to help them, so Issie grabbed Tokyo's lead rope and led the mare towards the hitching rail while Natasha tried to hold the hose with one hand and stick her other hand into the spout of cold water.

"It feels a little better," Natasha whimpered as Issie returned to her side.

"Keep holding it under the water," Issie told her. She grabbed a sponge out of her grooming kit. "Here," she said, "use this to wipe your hands to get the rest of it off."

"I think it's all gone," Natasha said a minute later, examining her hand in amazement. "Weird! My hand feels all numb and tingly!" She turned to Issie. "What the hell is in that stuff?"

"I don't know," Issie said. "But whatever it is, Verity has been putting it on our horses!"

After the drama with the liniment, Issie couldn't help telling Natasha about her own story, that first day at the stables when she saw Verity with the hypodermic needle.

"And you're sure she was actually injecting Tottie with it?" Natasha was astonished.

"Totally," Issie said. "I saw her do it."

"What do you think was in the syringe?"

"I don't know," Issie replied. "But after what happened to you today, I think we have to tell Ginty."

The two girls agreed that telling Ginty was the right thing to do. But it was no use trying to talk to her here at Sandilands. They knew that Ginty would be furious if they brought up something like this in front of Cassandra.

"We'll tell her in the truck on the way home," Issie assured Natasha. But this also proved impossible, as Verity had organised the seating again and made sure that she was the one sitting up front with Ginty.

It wasn't until they had got back to the stables and all the horses were unloaded and fed and Verity had gone home for the night that the pair finally got the chance.

They found Ginty in her office, sorting out paperwork. "Issie! Natasha!" Ginty said stiffly when she saw the girls in her doorway. "I thought you two would have gone home already. Why are you still here?"

"You tell her!" Natasha hissed.

"Why me?" Issie shot back. They were both losing their nerve.

"Because…" Natasha said, giving Issie a shove to make her step forward, "…it was your idea!"

"Issie?" Ginty was already fed up with the pair of them loitering in her doorway. "Do you have something you want to tell me?"

Issie nodded. "I… I don't want to tell tales on other riders, but after what happened today…"

"What happened? What are you talking about?" Ginty said. "This sounds serious."

"It is," Issie said. "It's about Verity. We think she's been giving something to the horses. I saw her the other day injecting Tottie with something and she said not to tell anyone. And then today she was putting that liniment on them and when Natasha touched it as we were washing the horses down afterwards it burnt her hand…"

As Issie explained everything that had happened, with Natasha standing beside her in mute agreement, Ginty listened intently. She sat behind her desk and absorbed the whole story and then she asked, "You two haven't spoken to anyone else about this?"

Issie shook her head. "We thought we should tell you first."

Ginty nodded sagely. "You did the right thing. I think it's best if we continue to keep this between ourselves. There could be talk on the circuit if word of this sort of thing got out."

"Oh, we won't tell anyone!" Natasha said. "Right, Issie?"

Issie nodded in agreement. Both of them could see Ginty's point. Gossip could get vicious, and if a rumour got out about Verity's behaviour, it could cause all sorts of trouble.

"Are you going to talk to Verity about it?" Issie asked nervously.

"Don't worry," Ginty said. "Leave it with me." There was an ominous chill in her voice as she added, "I'll deal with Verity."

Chapter 9

At 7 a.m. the next day the girls were in the loose boxes tacking up when they heard Ginty's voice booming out down the corridor. "Verity?" the trainer called. "In my office! Now!"

Issie and Natasha peered cautiously over the Dutch doors of their stalls as Verity walked past them towards Ginty, who was standing with her arms crossed waiting for her.

They watched as Ginty opened the office door and beckoned for Verity to come inside and then shut it firmly behind her.

"Come on!" Natasha said excitedly.

"What? What do you mean, *come on*?" Issie said,

horrified. "Where do you think you're going?"

"To listen to their conversation!" Natasha said. "Don't you want to hear what happens?"

"Of course I do, but—"

"Then stop being such a nana!" Natasha said. "Follow me!"

Natasha had been riding at Ginty's stables for long enough to know her way around the place. For instance, she knew that if you headed out the back door of the stables and went around through the gardens behind the scarlet hibiscus trees, you would end up beneath Ginty's office window. The two girls were hidden among the plants there, crouching down close enough to hear everything that was going on inside. Ginty was doing all the talking. She must have been pretty rough on Verity already, because the head groom was in tears and pleading with the trainer.

"I wasn't trying to cause trouble!" she told Ginty between sobs. "I just wanted Tottie to be OK—"

"Tottie is not your horse and these matters are not for you to decide," Ginty said with a distinctly frosty tone to her voice. "You have betrayed my trust. And your actions at the show yesterday put this whole stable at risk. If the showjumping federation inspectors heard rumours of doping you know what would happen. We'd be banned from competing!"

"What's going to happen to Tottie?" Verity sniffled. "And the others?"

"The horses are not your concern," Ginty told the head groom. "Verity, I'm afraid your behaviour leaves me with no other choice. Go back to the tack room and pack your bags. Your services here are no longer required. You can leave immediately."

Crouching beneath the window, Issie and Natasha looked at each other in total shock. What had they done? Verity had just been fired!

Training continued that day without Verity. It was a rest day for all the horses that had competed the day before and Issie, Natasha and Penny took three of Dulmoth Park's up-and-coming green four-year-olds who had only recently been broken to saddle out for a hack through the forest that backed on to Dulmoth Park's grounds. Being young, the horses were a little spooky at first, but once they were actually in the forest, they trotted quite happily in single file down the sandy paths that ran between the trees, with Penny taking the lead on a chestnut mare called Delta.

"What happened to Verity?" Penny asked now that they were out of earshot of the stables. "I saw her leaving Ginty's office in tears."

"Ginty fired her!" Natasha said. And before Issie could stop her, Natasha had blabbed the whole story about Verity doing strange things to the horses and Ginty telling her she had to go. Penny looked a little shocked, but she didn't seem upset.

"So what did Ginty say exactly?" she asked, eyes narrowing.

"We only caught the second half of the conversation," Natasha said, "but she was telling Verity that she couldn't have her around behaving like that and so she was, like, fired!"

Penny shook her head in amazement. "I hope Ginty's planning on replacing her. I'm not going to do all of Verity's work as extra for no more money!"

Before now, Issie had always assumed that Verity and Penny were best friends, but Penny's lack of sympathy made it clear that she couldn't have cared less. It reminded Issie of something that Verity had said on her very first day at Dulmoth Park. *You never know who your friends are around here.* She was right. A week ago Issie would never have believed she'd become friends with Natasha, but as they were riding home through the forest and Natasha was chatting away to her, Issie suddenly realised that the pair of them were actually getting along.

Ginty seemed to be in a better mood that afternoon too. She helped them to groom the horses that evening and do the hard feeds to make up for Verity's absence. They had finished feeding all the horses and Natasha and Penny had already gone home for the day when Ginty asked Issie to come back to her office "for a chat".

"You're aware of what happened this morning?" Ginty asked. "You know that I had to let Verity go?"

"Yes," Issie said nervously.

"Well, I'm going to need you to take over a couple of her horses to exercise them until we can find a replacement. And I'll need all of you to work extra hours to cover for her too."

"OK," Issie said.

"There's no extra money at this stage," Ginty paused. "But it's all valuable experience if you want a career as a rider, and I've got my eye on you for future promotion. Cassandra was very impressed by the way you rode Quebec. And even considering the problems you had with Flame, I think it was a good outing on the weekend. I think you'd fit in around here quite nicely if a permanent position ever came up." She reached into the top draw of her desk and handed Issie a brown envelope. "This is for you."

When Issie arrived home she was still clutching the envelope tightly in her hand.

"What's in there?" Mrs Brown asked.

"My first pay cheque," Issie said proudly. "Ginty called me in to her office to tell me that she's really happy with my work. She's giving me more responsibility too, now that Verity has gone."

And so, while Mrs Brown prepared their dinner, Issie filled her in on all the drama and Verity's departure.

"Ginty said that if I wanted, I could have a permanent

job at the stables in the future," Issie told her mother, unable to conceal her excitement.

Mrs Brown raised her eyebrows. "Well, I hope you told her that you couldn't take it. You're still at school."

"I know that!" Issie replied. "She didn't mean straight away. She meant when I leave school I could work there."

"Oh, Issie!" Mrs Brown sighed. "Do we have to keep having this argument? Horses are not a proper career. Maybe you can work there part-time while you're at university."

"I don't see why I need to go to university to be a professional rider," Issie grumbled.

"Wanting to be a professional rider when you grow up is like wanting to be a fairy princess," Mrs Brown said.

"Fairy princesses don't shovel horse poo at seven in the morning!" Issie pointed out with a grin.

Mrs Brown shook her head in amazement. "I have to admit I never thought you'd last at that place, getting up so early. I expected you to be begging me for a job in at the office by now!"

"I am pretty exhausted," Issie admitted. "Riding at least six horses a day takes it out of you."

"Have you got a favourite one yet?" Mrs Brown asked.

"Tokyo was my favourite, I guess – but I had to give her up for Natasha to ride," Issie said. "Now I'm riding this Hanoverian chestnut called Flame. He's really gorgeous and he has these amazing jumping bloodlines. He cost a fortune and he's supposed to be one of Ginty's stars, but he goes bonkers in the arena. He's got so much potential but he's a total nightmare. I can't figure him out."

"Maybe you could ask Tom to look at him?" Mrs Brown suggested.

"Yeah," Issie said sarcastically, "I'm sure Ginty would be thrilled if I did that."

"What do you mean?" Mrs Brown was taken aback.

"Ginty and Tom don't get on, Mum," Issie said. "Besides, she'd never let another instructor come and look at one of her horses."

Her mum didn't know anything about the way things worked in a professional stable, Issie thought. But Mrs Brown did have a point. Issie wished she could talk to Tom about Flame. She lay awake in bed for hours that night thinking about the big chestnut. What had made Flame perform so badly in the showjumping ring? She knew that with his bloodlines he could jump three times as high as the jumps in the arena, so it couldn't have been the size of the fences. Maybe it was the crowds that bothered him? Perhaps he needed an earguard like she used on Comet. Her Blackthorn Pony hated crowd noise when he jumped. This was the sort of idea she would have discussed normally with Avery, but when Issie offered her theory to Ginty the next morning at the stables, the red-haired instructor dismissed it briskly as nonsense.

"This horse simply needs to learn to do as he's told," she said stiffly. "He's had a day off to recover. Saddle him up and bring him into the arena. We're going to drill him and drill him until he gets it right."

The rapping session that day was even tougher than anything Issie had experienced before. Time and again, with Ginty barking the orders, Natasha and Penny lifted the rail up to bash Flame in the legs as Issie jumped him over.

"Hold him! Hold him!" Ginty shouted out at Issie with frustration. "Now go! Canter on!"

With each attempt at the jump, Flame became more strung out. He was charging the fences like a bull, his problems now getting worse, not better. Ginty kept telling Issie to hold him back, but this just drove the big chestnut into a frenzy. By the end of the day, instead of cantering on the spot as he had done at the competition the day before, the Hanoverian was cantering on the spot *and sideways*. He couldn't even look at the jumps without going berserk. It was like trying to ride a bucking bronco.

By the time Issie took Flame back to his stall, he was quivering all over and his whole body was wet with sweat. As Issie untacked the horse, she couldn't help but feel worried about him. Flame wasn't coping with the stress. She gave him his hard feed and tried to dry him off before she put his lightweight rug on him so that he could cool down.

"I'm sorry, boy," Issie said softly. "I'm trying to help, you know that, don't you?"

"Issie?" Ginty stuck her head over the partition. "Are you still in there? What's taking you so long? You should be saddling up your next ride by now."

"I'm just worried about Flame. I think maybe the training isn't right for him," Issie said. She realised it was the wrong thing to say as soon as it came out of her mouth. Ginty's face turned stony.

"I'm sure that when you're riding your pony-club ponies you coax them over the jumps with cuddles and carrots," Ginty said snidely, "but this is a professional stable, Issie. Horses need to learn how to work and do what is asked of them. And you need to learn to harden up. Flame is not a pet, he's an expensive investment."

"But if he's worth so much money, shouldn't we at least try—" Issie began, but Ginty cut her off.

"I have nearly thirty horses in work at these stables, Issie. They all respond to my training system. Flame will too. You need to do as I tell you."

Ginty seemed so confident of her methods. And she clearly didn't like being questioned. The trainer had a reputation for producing champion showjumpers, and compared to her, Issie was just some pony-club kid. What could she possibly know? But that was never how it had been with Avery. Issie had always been able to talk to Tom about her horses whenever she was in trouble. She only wished she could talk to him now.

It was late evening and the sky was turning a dusky pink colour on the horizon as Issie rode her bike up the driveway of Winterflood Farm.

It had only been three weeks ago that she'd had her argument with Avery, but it felt to Issie as if she hadn't been here for years. When she spotted Tom out the back with the horses she gave him a wave. Tom looked up and saw her and waved back. She couldn't tell at this distance whether he was pleased to see her or not. As he led the horse closer and came over to greet her she still wasn't sure. His face was expressionless.

Avery was leading a small pony, about twelve hands high, an Appaloosa with a very pretty blanket of white spots on its dark chocolate rump.

"Who's the new horse?" Issie asked.

"This is Cookie," Avery said. "He's a rescue pony. You should have seen the state of his feet when he arrived. He's quite sound again now – he'll be well enough and ready to be re-homed in a week or two." He looked at Issie, still in her jodhpurs and helmet after a hard day in the stables at Dulmoth Park. "Been at work?"

"Uh-huh," Issie nodded. "I thought I'd just drop in and say hi on my way home…"

This was patently untrue. Winterflood Farm wasn't on her way home. It was in completely the opposite direction. But if Avery knew she was lying, he didn't let on.

"Just let me give Cookie his feed," he smiled at her, "and we can have a cup of tea. I've just made a fruit loaf."

Five minutes later they were in the kitchen and Issie was telling Avery all about Flame rushing his jumps and getting crazy every time he was faced with even the tiniest fence.

Avery listened with a frown furrowing his brow. "Issie, I want to help, I really do, but I can't tell you what to do with someone else's horse…"

"I know that, Tom, but I thought we could at least talk about it. I keep thinking that his training isn't helping. We've been rapping him for the past two weeks—"

Avery froze. He stopped what he was doing and turned to face Issie again.

"Did you just say that Ginty is rapping him?"

"Uh-huh," Issie said. "She does it with all the horses."

"Issie, this is exactly why I didn't want you working for Ginty. I can't believe she's rapping the horses – it's a horrid practice – it should be outlawed."

"But Ginty said everyone does it! It's just a training technique."

"Some showjumping stables still do it," Avery admitted. "And sometimes it works. But it can be disastrous. For a horse like Flame all it does is make them lose their nerve, and then they become terrified every time they see a jump." He shook his head. "Besides it's cruel. I've seen horses that have been rapped until their legs bled. Not that Ginty would care. She's always been like this – willing to do whatever it takes to win."

"She's not like that!" Issie said, standing up for Ginty. "She actually fired one of her grooms for giving a horse an illegal injection! You don't know her! She really, really cares about the horses!"

"Oh, wake up, Issie!" Avery replied. "I know better than you exactly what Ginty is capable of. I've seen the damage that she's done in the past. She destroys good horses, and for some reason people pay her big money to do it." He looked Issie square in the eyes. "You can't stay on at the stables – she's mistreating those horses."

"What else am I supposed to do?" Issie asked.

"I don't know," Avery said, "but you can't continue working for her."

"But I can't just leave. Working in professional stables is what I've always dreamt of. Tom, she's talking about offering me a full-time job at Dulmoth Park once I leave school."

"You can't actually be considering it?" Avery was appalled.

Issie didn't know what to say. Did Avery really think that Ginty was so terrible that he wouldn't want Issie working for her? Even if it helped her to achieve her dream?

"I've gotta go," she said, standing up and putting down her slice of half-eaten fruit loaf. "Mum is expecting me for dinner." She walked out the door and grabbed her bike hastily, noticing that her hands were shaking as she wheeled it down the driveway.

"Issie, wait!" Avery called after her. But she pretended she didn't hear him as she clambered on quickly and leant hard against the pedals. She cycled like mad and managed to make it to the end of the driveway and out of Avery's sight, before she pulled over, her chest heaving, and burst into tears.

Chapter 10

When Issie arrived at the stables the next morning and saw that Flame was the first horse on her roster she felt sick at the prospect of trying to jump him again. She was hoping that maybe they'd be exercising the horses on a forest ride instead. But according to the roster they'd be working in the arena, where the jumps were set up at a substantial height ready for training.

Ginty hadn't managed to get another rider to replace Verity yet, but she did have two of the groundskeepers from Dulmoth Park on hand that morning helping out with the jumps. The two boys knew next to nothing about horses, but they had been given a brief explanation of what to do and now they stood by in position ready to lift the poles as Issie, Natasha and Penny began to warm their horses up, trotting round the arena.

"OK," Ginty called out to the riders. "Can I have you one at a time, please, over the jump where the boys are?"

Natasha went first. She was on Tokyo and the big bay mare picked her feet up neatly on the first try, but the boys had really yanked the pole up. They hit her hard, scraping the wood against her cannon bones and Issie saw Tokyo flinch as she tucked her legs up even higher.

Suddenly Issie knew that she couldn't go through with it. It was her turn, but how could she ride Flame over the jump knowing that the boys were going to hit him no matter what? Instead, she rode straight up to Ginty.

"I think these guys are hitting the horses too hard," she told her. "They've never done this before. They really bashed Tokyo with the rail just then."

"That's exactly what they're supposed to do," Ginty said flatly. "It was Tokyo's fault. She didn't lift her legs enough."

"But she did lift them."

Ginty ignored her. "It's your turn," she told Issie. "Take Flame in at a canter."

Issie didn't move.

"Is there a problem, Isadora?"

Issie nodded. "It's just that I've been talking to someone and this person told me that rapping is really cruel."

Ginty sighed. "This 'person' wouldn't be Tom Avery, would it?"

"Ummmm..." Issie hesitated.

"It's all right," Ginty said, "I'm not expecting you to compromise your loyalty to him. I know that Avery is your friend. And I have nothing against him and his methods – but he seems to be obsessed with me!"

Ginty's expression looked sorrowful, as if she were deeply hurt by Avery's accusations. "What can I say? Avery's a pony-club instructor and I'm a professional. He probably can't stand the fact that I've had more champion showjumpers than he's had hot dinners. For some reason he seems to think that must mean that I'm doing something naughty."

Ginty held Flame's reins and reached out and stroked

the chestnut's glossy neck. "Isadora, I am the best in the business. And that isn't just because of my methods, it's also about instincts. I have an eye for a good horse." Then Ginty reached her bony hand out and grasped Issie's hand in her own. "I have an eye for a good rider too. I have big plans for you, Issie. I like the way you ride. I think you could go a long way in this business and become a very good professional rider one day, hopefully working for my stables."

Issie couldn't help but feel flattered at this. "I tried to explain to Tom. I told him it's a professional stable and things are different, but he didn't listen…"

Ginty nodded, her face filled with understanding. "Isadora, it's hard for a man like him to change. It's been a long time since he rode at Badminton. Tom's stuck in his old ways. He's not exposed to new ideas and techniques the way you and I are on the competition circuit."

Ginty kept her hand tightly clasped around Issie's and looked deep into her eyes as she spoke. "He's trying to hold you back, Issie. Can't you see that? Avery is desperate. He doesn't want to lose you."

Her voice was firm now and her grip tightened as

she said, "Sometimes the best pupils outgrow their teachers. Isn't it time for Tom to face the fact that he has to let you go?"

Ginty was right. Issie wasn't a pony-club kid any more. She had responsibilities at the stables and her riding had become a serious business. Avery didn't understand. Neither did her friends. On Tuesday when Stella phoned her up and asked Issie if she wanted to go for a ride after work the next day, she had to make an excuse and say she couldn't make it. Riding more horses was the last thing Issie felt like doing after being at the stables all day.

"How about Thursday, then?" Stella suggested. "Kate wants to come too – we haven't seen you in ages!"

"It's only been a couple of weeks," Issie said.

"Well, that's ages!" Stella laughed. Then she made another suggestion. "On Friday we're going to have a lesson with Tom. We could ask him to make it at five to give you time to get there once you finish at work?"

"I don't think that would work out," Issie said,

thinking about her last conversation with Avery. "I can't make it, Stella. I'm sorry. With Verity gone, we all have to cover for her and I have loads of extra work. I'm too busy."

It was true that she had extra work to do at Dulmoth Park. Issie was riding seven or eight horses most days. Flame was still behaving badly and Issie seemed to spend all her time in the arena fighting with the big chestnut. Her worst moment was during another rapping lesson on Wednesday when Flame got so over the top he simply ran through the entire course, demolishing all the jumps!

Ginty decided that he needed more aerobic exercise to take the edge off his high spirits and so the riders spent Thursday and Friday taking the horses out into the forest for big, long rides with lots of trotting to work off their excess energy. Verity still hadn't been replaced, but the others hardly noticed her absence. Issie found herself actually enjoying the extra responsibility too. Ginty would spend some time with her each morning explaining a different aspect of stable care. Instead of being baffled by the huge array of feeds and supplements that the horses were given, Issie now knew each of the thirty horses' diet plans off by heart. She could icepack tired legs and apply a cooling clay poultice without thinking twice. And there wasn't a piece of equipment in the tack room that she didn't know how to use.

The atmosphere in the stable was more cheerful and relaxed with Verity gone, too. Issie had thought that Natasha might wig out and get jealous that Issie was taking on some of Verity's main responsibilities, but she remained in a good mood. Natasha was happy with the six horses that she had been assigned to ride, and she couldn't have given a hoot as long as she didn't have to do extra work.

On the Saturday morning Issie rose at four thirty, even earlier than usual. It hardly seemed worth going to bed when you were getting up like this in the middle of the night, Issie thought. But that was the life of a professional rider. Today they were taking seven of the horses to the Westfields show. It was a two-hour drive to get there so they needed to leave by 6 a.m. That meant having all the horses ready to be loaded with their gear before it got light.

At the stables, Issie did the hard feeds before anything else. She fed Flame last and stood there watching as the big chestnut snuffled down his feed.

"You're going to go well today," Issie said softly to the horse, "I know you are…"

"Issie?" It was Natasha. "I think you need to come and take a look at Tottie."

Tottie was one of Issie's horses now, and for the past week she had been riding the grey mare every day. She'd jumped the mare on Thursday over some low fences just to get a feel for her, and on Friday she'd taken her on a long road hack. Tottie had been fine then, in fact the mare was so fit she was a bit above herself, pulling hard and wanting to canter the whole way home. But that morning was quite different. Tottie was standing quietly in the corner and when Natasha went in and led her over towards the door Issie could see straight away that she was favouring a leg.

"It's her near-hind," she said. "She's really sore on it."

"What shall we do?" Natasha asked.

"Don't bother to put her floating boots on," Issie said. "She won't be going anywhere. She can't compete like that."

"OK," Natasha nodded.

"I'll tell Ginty that there are only going to be six horses for the truck," Issie said.

Ginty's reaction, however, was not at all what Issie expected.

"Put her protective gear on and load her on-board," Ginty said firmly.

"But she's lame—" Issie began. Ginty ignored her and grabbed the paperwork off her office desk, barging past and leaving Issie in her wake.

"Load her on the truck," she said darkly over her shoulder, as she headed off towards the stables. "And don't question me again."

"But what's the point of loading her up if she's lame?" Natasha asked when Issie told her what Ginty had said.

"I don't know," Issie said as she Velcroed Tottie's floatboots on to her hind legs. "But I do know I'm not saying anything to her about it again. She's the boss. If she wants to take a lame horse to the show, that's her business."

Aside from Ginty's frosty behaviour over Tottie, the trainer seemed to be in good spirits. She laughed and joked with the girls as they loaded the horses on the truck for the long drive to the Westfields grounds. Natasha and Penny were in the back with the horses this time and Issie rode up front in the cab with Ginty.

It was the first time Issie had really had the chance to talk to her boss, and she found herself telling the trainer all about her own horses. Not just Comet and Blaze, but Nightstorm too. Ginty was fascinated when Issie told her about Blaze's son, and how the colt was in Spain right now, training with the famed Spanish Andalusians, learning *haute école* dressage under the direction of the mysterious Francoise D'arth.

"He sounds like a very special young horse," Ginty said.

"He really is," Issie said wistfully. "I miss him so much, but it was the right thing to do, leaving him there at El Caballo Danza Magnifico. Francoise has promised that one day, when Nightstorm's training is completed, he'll be returned to me. It's just that sometimes it feels like that day is never going to come."

Ginty told a few stories of her own about her showjumping exploits over the years and her early days as a competitive rider.

"I would load up five horses by myself and head off to a show," she told Issie. "Most of them were green good-for-nothings that I'd bought cheap. I'd clean them up, clip them and rug them, give them a good groom, pull their manes and plait them. I'd put a month of effort into schooling them up and then I'd take them to the shows, win a few ribbons and flick them on for a few thousand and turn a tidy profit. That was the way I got started in this business. It was hard graft, but eventually I had enough money and enough of a reputation behind me to get owners who wanted to sponsor me. After that I could afford the better horses and success quickly followed."

Ginty looked out of the window at the road ahead. "I dragged myself up by my bootstraps. I've worked hard for everything I've got..." Issie saw a cold expression on the trainer's face as she added, "Only the tough survive in this game – and winning is everything."

It was almost 8 a.m. when Ginty finally drove the truck into the showgrounds and already the place was filling up fast with competitors' floats and trucks.

The girls unloaded the horses, unwrapped their tail bandages, took off floating boots and began to groom them. They knew the ropes now and Ginty didn't need to tell them what to do. By eight thirty they were almost ready, so Ginty sent her three riders off to walk the showjumping course.

There were four rings set up at Westfields. Issie was riding Flame in the novice hack ring and Quebec in the pony ring, and had been entered in the open hack ring on Tottie – not that she was actually expecting to ride the mare now that she was lame.

Natasha had Tokyo as her open ride and also Baxter, who had been entered along with Quebec in the pony ring. Penny was riding Vertigo in the open class and would also ride Sebastian.

"Since we've all got a horse entered in the open classes, let's walk that course together, and then we can split up and you can walk the other rings by yourselves," Penny suggested.

The open ring was a big course, which was to be expected. The jumps were already set at a metre twenty for the first class of the day and by the end of the day they would be as high as a metre fifty. Penny guided the girls through the fences on foot, and they discussed striding and alternative routes to get around the ring in a faster time. Issie spent all of her time just trying to remember which jump came next. She had to remember three courses that day! That was the thing about riding professionally. If you had more than one horse and more than one course to remember it could get jumbled in your head.

"You'll get used to it," Penny told her. "It helps if you imagine yourself actually riding around the fences rather than just walking between them."

As Issie and Natasha entered the pony ring, Issie tried to keep Penny's advice in mind. She imagined she could feel herself gathering her pony up underneath her, finding her line, and then pushing on at the jump. She was halfway around the course, riding with her mind and trying to find the right striding as she came up to the second element of the double, when Aidan appeared in front of her.

"Hi," he grinned, "fancy seeing you here!"

Issie smiled back. "You just ruined my clear round."

"What?"

"I was riding my imaginary horse. I was halfway to a clear round, but now I'm lost again," Issie explained.

"I prefer riding real ones myself," Aidan said.

"Are you on Fortune today?" Issie asked.

"Yep, and I'm riding another two ponies for Araminta as well."

"So I'll see you in the ring then?" Issie said.

"Why don't you come and see me for lunch too?" Aidan smiled. "We didn't really get the chance to catch up last week."

"I know," Issie sighed. She looked over at Natasha, who was mouthing at her to hurry up. "I... I really need to get going," Issie told Aidan. "We need to get back to the truck and get the horses ready."

"So," Aidan said, "meet me at lunchtime then?"

"I can't," Issie said. "Ginty doesn't like us hanging out with other riders. She wants the team to stay together."

"You're kidding!" Aidan frowned. "It's your lunch break. You should be able to do whatever you like."

"I *can* do what I like," Issie asserted.

"So you're saying you don't want to have lunch with me? Is that it?"

"No," Issie said, "it's just that I'm working and I don't want to upset Ginty."

"So you're scared of her?"

"No!" Issie was getting upset now. Why did Aidan

insist on getting the wrong end of the stick? "It's not like that. I just want to be professional."

"Being a professional doesn't mean not having any fun or any friends," Aidan shot back.

"What do you mean?" Issie said. "I can't believe this is all because I won't have lunch with you."

"It's not just lunch," Aidan said. "It's more than that. It's about how you've been acting lately. I met up with Stella and Kate for a lesson at Avery's the other day and they said you've hardly spoken to them since you started working for Ginty. Like you're too good to hang out with your old friends now you're riding on the showjumping circuit."

Issie was taken aback. "Stella said that about me?"

Aidan shook his head. "Stella would never talk about you behind your back. But I could tell she was really hurt. She said she's asked you loads of times to go riding after work and you always say no."

"I work long hours," Issie mumbled, "and I'm tired at the end of the day. I don't really feel like hacking about pointlessly..."

The words slipped out before she realised what she was saying. She saw Aidan's face fall. "Well, if that's how you feel, I won't keep you from your important work any longer," he said. "I'm a professional too, you know. I better get back to my horses."

"Aidan, no! I didn't mean it like that…" Issie called after him. But he ignored her and walked away.

"Come on, Issie!" Natasha was beside her, jumping about with such urgency it looked as if she was dying to go to the loo. "We need to get back to the truck. Ginty will kill us if we're late!"

Issie walked back to the truck in a state of shock. Why did Aidan have to fight with her now? He had ruined her course walk and she would never remember her route. Come to think of it, did Aidan have to fight with her at all? It was none of his business if Issie was too busy to see her friends. He had no idea what it was like trying to juggle her work and everything else. The more she thought about it, the more furious she became, and by the time they had reached the horse truck she was full of righteous indignation. She'd done nothing wrong. She was just doing her job.

She was so cross about Aidan, it took her a moment to focus on what was happening right in front of her eyes. Tottie had been saddled up and put on the lunge rein.

Ginty was lunging her now at a trot in a twenty-metre circle right beside the horse truck. Issie and Natasha watched slack-jawed as the mare trotted briskly around the circle.

"I don't believe it," Natasha whispered.

"Me neither," Issie said.

The grey mare was lifting up her hooves neatly, her head held high. As she trotted freely on the lunge there was no sign of the soreness that had been there earlier that morning.

"It's a miracle," Natasha said.

Issie had to agree. Tottie was no longer lame.

Chapter 11

Tottie's lameness had completely disappeared and the mare performed like a superstar, winning ribbons in two classes. Flame, meanwhile, was a nightmare ride. At times, when Issie could get the powerful chestnut under control, she could see hints of the greatness that lay deep within him. His jump was so scopey, that even when he was approaching the fences in his crazy, overexcited crab-step and pulling at the reins like mad, he could still fly the fences with ease. But his ability was marred by inconsistency. Again and again Issie managed to get him jumping neatly, only to have him go completely berserk if he so much as brushed a rail with his legs, behaving as if he had been given an electric shock. He'd then lose his cool so badly that he'd go on to bowl through the next jump and bring the whole fence down.

Back at the horse truck, Ginty brushed off Issie's concerns. "He's your responsibility," she snapped. "Pull your socks up and start riding him properly or I'll get Penny to ride him instead!"

Issie was horrified. It wasn't her fault that Flame was going so badly, was it?

"Ginty doesn't care whose fault it is," Natasha told her bluntly. "She just doesn't want to be embarrassed in front of Cassandra. You're making her look bad."

Natasha was right. Ginty was hellbent on impressing Cassandra – especially since today she had just asked the millionairess to spend even more money buying another new horse for the stable. But Flame was hardly proving to be a great advertisement. Ginty tried to keep Cassandra away from the ringside so that she wouldn't see the chaos Flame was causing on the jumping course. But it all went wrong when Cassandra happened to catch sight of the chestnut gelding crashing his way through his final round for the day.

Cassandra was less than impressed and she told

Ginty that there would be no buying of a new horse. "I think you've got enough on your plate with this one, haven't you?" she said.

Ginty didn't seem to have any answers to Flame's problems. Her only solution seemed to be rubbing copious amounts of some new kind of liniment into his legs between classes. Though heaven knew what good that was supposed to do, Issie thought. The horse's problem wasn't that his legs were stiff – it was that he continued to act bonkers in the ring.

Flame was a washout in all five of his classes that day and Issie's only success in the hack ring was a first and second place on Tottie. Penny, meanwhile, had done well on Vertigo and Sebastian and won two of her classes.

In the pony ring, however, Team Araminta were definitely the ones who came out on top. Aidan and Morgan had beaten both Issie and Natasha in most of the events, with Fortune performing like a total hero. The partnership won all four of their classes that day. Issie had managed to mumble a "well done" to Aidan as she joined him in the arena to collect her blue second-place sash while he received the red ribbon yet again. Aidan responded with a polite "thank you". But that was the only time they spoke.

At lunchtime, Issie kept thinking that Aidan might come over and apologise for the way he had talked to her that morning, but he didn't appear. Then before she knew it the afternoon's competition was winding up and they were loading the horses back on the truck and heading for Dulmoth Park.

It had been a long day, and it wasn't over yet. Ginty asked Issie to stay on to do all the hard feeds and ice Tottie's legs as well. It was late when Issie finally left the stables and headed for home. The bike ride back was the final straw at the end of a tough day, and she was aching and exhausted by the time she got to the front door.

"At last! I'm keeping the dinner warm in the oven," Mrs Brown told her as she walked in. "Go get changed out of your jods and I'll dish it up."

Issie was hardly great company that evening. She sat at the table lost in her own world, picking at her reheated casserole, still hurting over her conversation with Aidan. He didn't have the right to talk to her like that! He couldn't tell her what to do. Why did everyone seem to have an opinion on her working for Ginty? It wasn't like she had many options if she wanted to be a professional rider around here. Apart from maybe Araminta, there was no one else in Chevalier Point who had the resources that Ginty had.

Avery certainly didn't. Winterflood Farm was nice enough with its neat green hedges and small stable block, but it was low-powered and impoverished compared to Dulmoth Park. A single one of those Hermès saddles in Ginty's tack room was probably worth more than all of Avery's tack put together! Issie was only realising now just how much money mattered when you were talking about professional riding. If she was really serious about being a competitive international rider one day then she was going to need a backer, someone like Cassandra with enough money to provide her with the high-class horses required to take her to the top.

"Too rich for you?"

"What?" Issie was startled.

"The casserole," Mrs Brown said pointing to Issie's untouched plate. "Is it too rich? Or are you not hungry?"

Issie shook her head. "It's fine, Mum. I just had a tough day."

"What do you mean?" Mrs Brown looked worried.

"Things aren't going very well with Flame. He went bonkers today in the ring." Issie sighed. "Plus I had a fight with Aidan at the show. I don't think we're speaking any more."

"A fight?" said Mrs Brown. "What about?"

"It was, well, it wasn't a fight really. He just said some things…" Issie paused. "Mum? Do you think I've changed since I started working for Ginty?"

"Is that what Aidan said to you?"

Issie nodded. "I just feel like my life has suddenly got really complicated. It used to just be me and my horses and Stella and Kate, but now I've got all this pressure on me…"

Mrs Brown put her arm around her daughter. "Do you remember your first day at pony club? I think you'd only had Mystic for a couple of weeks and you were so excited to be in your new uniform with your own pony. The look on your face! I'd never seen you so happy. You loved that grey pony so much, you couldn't stand to be apart from him. After the rally was over you didn't want to come home. You would have stayed at the paddock all night with him if I'd let you. As far as you were concerned, it was just you and your horse, and the world didn't matter. And now here you are four years later and it's not just you and your pony any more. You've got responsibility for a whole stable-full of horses and suddenly it's all serious and frightfully grown-up…"

Mrs Brown paused for a moment. "But I still see the same look in your eyes, Issie. It's that look you had when you rode for the first time. It proves that no matter how complicated your world has become, the girl that you are inside is still the same." Mrs Brown smiled at her daughter. "You love horses as much as you ever did, and that will never change. No matter what anyone says."

Issie collapsed into bed exhausted at nine o'clock, thrilled that tomorrow was Sunday and for once she didn't need to set the alarm for 6 a.m. She had somehow been talked into working a seven-day week for Ginty, but at least tomorrow the trainer had agreed to let her have a lie-in and she didn't have to start work until eight. She was determined to leave Dulmoth Park on the dot of four so she could head down to the River Paddock to give Blaze and Comet some much-needed exercise. She had been neglecting her horses lately because of work, and she needed to make time for them again.

Her lie-in never happened. Instead, she woke up at two o'clock in the middle of the night, startled from her sleep by noise down below her bedroom window in the garden.

It was Wombat. The blue heeler pup always slept downstairs, on a dog bed on the back porch by the French doors. It was a common occurrence for the pup to wake Issie with his fussing and whimpering because he'd found a hedgehog curled in a prickly ball on the lawn.

Issie knew that she'd better get out there straight away and get Wombat. Not that the hedgehog needed her help. Wombat was usually the one who usually came off the worst in these tussles and ended up with a bleeding snout for his troubles!

She got out of bed and slipped on her jods and a pair of trainers, grabbed her Dulmoth Park sweatshirt, which was sitting on top of her laundry pile, pulled it on over her pyjama top and padded downstairs.

In the kitchen, Issie stared out through the glass of the French doors looking for her pup. She could hear Wombat growling, but when she scanned the lawn she couldn't see him or his prickly prey. All she saw outside were the shadows of the big trees that spread out over the lawn. She reached up a hand to open the top lock on the door when she saw something that made her freeze. That was why Wombat was growling! One of the shadows was moving! It was a big shape too – much too big to be a dog. Issie didn't move. She watched the shadow move closer, and then, as she recognised the silhouette in the moonlight, she let out a sigh of relief and began once again to frantically work the lock.

The moment she stepped outside, Wombat ran to her. The hackles on his back were raised and he was still growling, a low threatening rumble coming from his throat. Issie smiled at the dog's devotion to protecting her, and crouched down beside him, one arm hugging his neck as she gave him a reassuring pat.

"Shush!" she told the dog. "Don't growl, Wombat.

You'll wake Mum." Then she looked up at the shadow standing on the lawn in front of them. "It's OK. It's all right, boy, he's not dangerous."

Wombat didn't seem convinced. He pressed himself against Issie's legs, the growl still rumbling through him as he stared at the shadowy shape standing right in front of them.

"Wombat! Don't be a silly puppy!" Issie tried to coax the dog forward as she walked into the darkness towards the shadow. "Come and meet Mystic."

Mystic didn't seem at all concerned by the blue heeler's antics. He stood calmly on the lawn, illuminated by the moonlight, waiting for Issie to come to him.

Issie stepped forward with Wombat trailing anxiously behind her. She wasn't certain what it was about Mystic that had the pup so rattled. Could Wombat remember Mystic from that night in Australia with the wild dog? Probably not – the pup was barely conscious when Mystic had arrived to save them. Maybe Wombat simply wasn't expecting a horse to appear in the back garden in the middle of the night. Or was it because the pup could sense somehow that this horse had an otherworldly quality to him, that he wasn't really supposed to be here at all?

Issie remembered her own shock the very first time she encountered Mystic here after the accident. She understood that her pony shouldn't be here, but at the same time she knew he was real. She never for a moment questioned Mystic's return. All she knew was that each time she saw him her heart soared to have her pony back with her once more.

There was a catch, of course. Mystic's arrival tonight meant that there was trouble. So, overjoyed as she was to see the grey gelding, Issie knew that there would be a darker reason for this late-night visit.

"Come on, Wombat," Issie cooed. The blue heeler had finally summoned up his courage and joined Issie on the lawn. Now he reached up his snout so that he was nose to nose with the pony. Mystic gave a stomp with his front hoof and Wombat leapt back again, cowering against Issie's legs. Issie giggled.

"He won't hurt you, Wombat," she said, "but you better stay here. Mystic and I have to go now."

Wombat was well-trained. He knew exactly what Issie meant when she said 'stay' — he just chose to ignore her. If there was an adventure afoot then he was coming too! As Issie led the grey pony down to the gate at the end of the back lawn, Wombat disobeyed her command and ran after her. He caught up by the time they had reached the back gate.

"OK," Issie sighed. "Have it your way, Wombat. I don't have time to argue." She let the pup go through the gate ahead of them, then guided Mystic through and asked him to stand still as she climbed the gate rungs and threw herself on to his back.

The pony waited expectantly as she arranged herself comfortably and grabbed a tangle of his thick mane in her hands. The mane wasn't for steering purposes, it was only to help her hang on and keep her balance. Not that she was the one doing the steering. Mystic would decide where to go. The grey pony had turned up tonight for her and he alone knew where they were heading.

As they set off at a trot along the narrow road that ran behind her house, Wombat was following them determinedly, running alongside Mystic. The dog's mouth was hanging open in that wide grin that pups get when they are enjoying a run, and his dark eyes shone brightly. He was excited by this night-time adventure. Issie was excited too, but there was a sense of foreboding as well. She had no clue as to why Mystic had turned up tonight. And she had no idea what was in store.

A little further down the road they reached an intersection, and when Mystic turned left Issie realised they must be heading in the direction of the pony club. She didn't understand why they'd be going there. Blaze and Comet were both grazing at the River Paddock.

Her confusion became even greater when they reached the club gates but Mystic didn't turn down the gravel driveway. He kept going past the club, cantering along the grass verge.

The road beyond the club gates was familiar to her. It was the same route she took every morning on her bicycle when she rode to work. She understood where Mystic was taking her now. They were going to Dulmoth Park.

Mystic was far faster down this road than Issie was on her bike and they were at the gates in just a few minutes. The entrance was shut tight, but Issie knew the code off by heart. She leant down from Mystic's back to punch the letters into the blue-lit keypad. Wombat raced eagerly through the entrance ahead of her as soon as the electronic gates glided open. She followed after him on Mystic, heading towards the black outline of the stables in the distance.

The main door to the stable entrance was open. Issie slid down from Mystic's back and left him at the doorway as she walked inside.

It was even darker in here than it was outside. The cavernous space of the main corridor was full of echoes as the horses moved restlessly in their stalls. At her side, Wombat gave a low growl.

"It's OK, boy," she reassured the pup. "No need to get spooked, it's just the horses."

There was a tremble to Issie's voice as she spoke to her dog. It was creepy in here at night. She would have turned on the lights, but they were at the other end of the corridor by the feed room. The corridor was almost pitch-black and Issie kept imagining that she saw things moving in the darkness.

When she was halfway down the corridor, she was

suddenly convinced that there was someone standing in the shadows by one of the stalls watching her. She spun round to confront them, her heart racing, only to realise that it was a pitchfork leant up against the wall.

"Ohmygod!" Issie clutched at her chest with her hands. Then she leant down and whispered to Wombat. "I'm being silly and freaking myself out. There's no one else here—"

She stopped in mid-sentence. A light had just been switched on in the feed room at the far end of the corridor! This wasn't about spooking at shadows any more. There was definitely someone else here!

Beside her, in the darkness, Wombat began to growl again. It was a tremulous growl, much more anxious than the low rumble he'd made in the backyard at home. The dog had seen the light come on too, and now he could hear noises at the far end of the corridor. Whoever was in the feed room was crashing and banging about. What was going on?

The deep rumble in Wombat's chest became louder and then the blue heeler gave a warning bark. "Shush!" Issie said. She put out a hand to hold the dog back, but

Wombat was too quick. Before she could get a hand on him he was running towards the feed room.

"Wombat! Wait!" Issie ran after him, but the dog was twice as fast as she was. His barking echoed down the corridor and Issie felt a sick wave of panic rising up in her. Wombat had no idea what he was dealing with! The pup could be in terrible danger!

"Wombat!" She raced down the corridor and ran panting through the doorway.

The room was empty. The only sign that anyone had been there at all was the storage locker shaped like a treasure chest – the lock on the lid had been forced and the box was wide open. Wombat was standing beside the treasure chest and his eyes were glued to the stack of horse blankets in the corner of the room. He was snarling, his teeth bared.

"What is it, Wombat?" Issie's voice came out wobbly. She could already see what the dog was growling at. There was a figure crouching low, cowering behind the horse blankets.

"I can see you back there!" Issie said, trying to keep the tremor out of her voice as she spoke again. "Don't move. I'm going to call the police!"

"No! Please. Don't! Issie – it's me!"

The figure emerged from behind the horse blankets. Issie could see that it was a girl immediately, but it wasn't until the intruder pulled back the hood on her sweatshirt that Issie saw her face.

It was Verity.

Chapter 12

Verity! Wombat stopped growling as soon as he recognised the girl and his tail began to wag. Issie, on the other hand, remained utterly defensive. She saw no reason to trust Dulmoth Park's former head groom.

"You shouldn't be here," Issie said. "It's the middle of the night."

"I know it looks bad," Verity walked closer towards Issie, "but really, I can explain…"

Wombat began to growl again as Verity edged close and Issie started backing away. She was shuffling backwards nervously, heading for the door, when she looked down and saw a bottle lying on the floor. "How did this get here…" Issie began to say. Then she realised that there were more bottles just like it scattered on the ground beside the storage chest. "Ohmygod!" Issie murmured.

The chest was like a vet's clinic – it was absolutely full of bottles of pills, syringes and tubs of liniment! Bottles and vials of fluid were strewn everywhere. Verity had obviously been rummaging through the contents when Wombat had interrupted her.

"What is all this stuff?" Issie asked.

"Phenylbutazone, capsaicin, pep pills… Ginty's secret medicine stash," Verity replied.

"Ginty's medicine stash?" Issie was confused. "What do you mean? You're the one who was injecting Tottie! And using the liniment! I saw you. Ginty fired you for it!"

"Is that what you think?" Verity looked at Issie as if she were a total idiot. "Oh man, this is so lame. You really don't know what's going on here at all!"

"What do you mean?" Issie frowned.

"Ginty didn't fire me because I was using drugs on the horses," Verity said. "She got rid of me because I *wouldn't do it* any more. She wanted me to keep giving Tottie the injections. That day at the Sandilands show she asked me to inject Tottie again, and I told her it was over and I refused to be involved. It didn't do any good of course – she must have injected Tottie herself anyway. All it did was get me fired."

Verity stepped over towards Issie and picked up one of the glass vials out of the medicine chest and handed it to Issie.

"This is what she's been injecting Tottie with."

Issie looked at the bottle. It had the word **phenylbutazone** written on the label in big, black letters.

"I've never heard of this stuff," Issie said.

"Horsey people don't call it by its full name," Verity said. "It's usually just called bute. It masks lameness in horses. If you put bute in their hard feed or inject them with it the pain goes away."

"So it cures them?" Issie was confused.

"No." Verity shook her head. "It doesn't cure them at all. They still have the same problems and bute won't make them well again. It just numbs them so they can't feel the pain any more. It stops them from looking lame – temporarily at least."

Issie was beginning to understand. "When I saw

you injecting Tottie, that was bute you were using, wasn't it?"

Verity nodded. "Tottie has arthritis. The bute is supposed to help ease her pain. But Ginty is using too much – and she's making Tottie jump even though she's really lame and needs to rest. Her bones can't take the stress. I tried to tell Ginty that we should spell her, rest her for a few weeks, but she wouldn't listen to me. She wants to keep Tottie pumped up full of bute to mask her symptoms for the rest of the season so that Dulmoth Park can win the accumulator championship with her. After that, Tottie would be worth a fortune and Ginty could sell her on for loads of money before anyone realised she had problems."

"So what were you doing here tonight?" Issie said. "Were you going to inject her again?"

"Ohmygod – no!" Verity was horrified. "If Ginty keeps up this regime Tottie is going to break down!" She looked genuinely distraught. "I came here to take everything in the medicine chest. I was going to get rid of the drugs so she couldn't use them any more. She's got to be stopped, Issie. You have to believe me – Ginty is dangerous. I'm telling you the truth!"

Issie didn't know what to think. "Just because you and Ginty don't agree on the best way to manage Tottie—" she began.

"Tottie?" Verity shook her head. "This isn't just about Tottie. Issie – open your eyes! Ginty is doping all the horses."

"You're wrong," Issie said defensively. "She isn't giving bute to Flame."

"No, she isn't," Verity agreed. Then she reached a hand into the chest and pulled out a tub of Ginty's liniment. "She's using this."

"That's horse liniment," Issie said obstinately.

Verity undid the lid on the tub. "Come here then!" she commanded Issie.

"What?" Issie didn't move.

"If you're so sure that this is just horse liniment," Verity said, "then you won't mind if I put some on your hand."

She reached out to grab Issie's hand, but Issie pulled back from her. "No. Don't put it on me, I know what it feels like – it's like your skin is burning. That's the stuff that Natasha got on her hand."

Verity nodded. "It's called capsaicin. Ginty uses it

to make the horses pick their feet up when they jump."

"How does it make them do that?"

"Have you ever had a really spicy meal with chilli in it and felt like your tongue was on fire?" Verity asked. "That's the same stuff that's in this jar. Capsaicin is made from hot chilli peppers and when you rub it on the horses' legs it makes them super-sensitive. The slightest sensation feels like fire on their skin. Once you've put on the capsaicin they won't want their legs to graze the jumps because it hurts too much."

Issie thought back to the last show at Westfields, when Ginty had slathered on the cream in between each jumping competition.

"Poor Flame!" Issie was appalled. "No wonder he's been freaking out in the ring."

Verity nodded. "With some horses, capsaicin can make them pick their feet up. But it's dangerous and other horses can just totally wig out – like Flame. It must really hurt him every time he touches a rail."

"Why didn't Ginty tell me that she was using it on him?" Issie asked.

"Because capsaicin is totally illegal," Verity said.

"They disqualified riders at the Olympics when they caught them using it. They even have machines to scan horses' legs for it now. If they find it in a horse's bloodstream then that horse and rider are banned from competing."

Issie couldn't believe it. "But Ginty uses that stuff like it's water! She's constantly rubbing it on all the horses. If this is true then you need to go to the police. Tell them what you've just told me!"

Verity shook her head. "Ginty fired me for injecting the horses, remember? I'm the one that looks like the criminal here. Besides, the police don't care about horses being injected with bute. It might be illegal to use it in competitions, but it's not like it's illegal to use it full stop. Lots of people use bute on their horses."

"But if lots of people use it," Issie said, "then maybe Ginty is just doing what she thinks is best for the horses?"

"You know that's not true. All she cares about is winning and keeping her rich owners happy. She's out of control, and she's got to be stopped." Verity's voice was cold. "I told you when you came here, didn't I? It's impossible to know who to trust. Well it's time to make up your mind, Issie. Whose side are you on?"

Issie hesitated and didn't say anything at first. Verity gave her a despairing look then pushed past her and reached down to pick up the bottles of medicine that were lying on the ground.

"Don't." Issie grabbed her hand to stop her. "If Ginty catches you doing this, you'll be in even more trouble."

"I'm taking all this stuff with me," Verity insisted.

"You can't, that's stealing. She'd call the police and they'd never believe you." Issie looked at Verity. "You'd better leave."

"And what are you going to do?" Verity asked.

Issie took a deep breath. "I think you're right. It's time for me to decide whose side I'm on."

After Verity had gone, Issie went back outside to look for Mystic, but the grey pony was already long gone. Issie had no way to get home so she decided to stay at the stables until Ginty arrived. The clock in the feed room said four thirty, and it wouldn't be long until dawn. Issie lay down on the horse blankets in the corner to have a little rest. But she was so exhausted, she found her eyelids getting heavy. The stack of horse blankets was quite soft and too cosy to resist and when Wombat snuggled in beside her she must have dozed off. When she woke up it was turning light outside. She could hear footsteps in the corridor, and the next thing she knew Ginty was walking into the feed room.

"Issie!" Ginty looked shocked at the sight of her and Issie suddenly realised she must look quite odd, curled up with her dog on a pile of horse rugs.

"What's been going on in here?" the flame-haired trainer demanded. Then she caught sight of the medicine chest. Issie had tried to tidy it up a bit last night, but there were still a couple of bottles on the floor that she'd missed and the lock was broken open.

Issie stood up. "Verity was here, at the stables."

Ginty stopped dead. "What? When?"

"Last night," Issie said.

Ginty frowned. "Well, I can see I'm going to have to change the code on the front gate..." She hurried forward to pack the remaining bottles back into the medicine chest. "Did she take anything?" she asked.

"No," Issie shook her head. "But she told me about

what you did to the horses, how you've been using capsaicin on Flame and the others. She said it wasn't her – that it was you that was injecting the bute into Tottie."

Issie held her breath, hoping that the trainer would be shocked at the accusation. But Ginty didn't so much as blink. So it was true! She had been doping the horses!

"Verity told me that if you don't stop, Tottie will break down," Issie said.

"That's her ill-informed opinion, is it?" Ginty replied sharply. "Frankly, you could fit Verity's total knowledge of horse treatment into my little finger. She doesn't know what she's talking about." Ginty looked squarely at Issie. "None of my riders have the right to question my methods. I think I've made that quite clear."

"You have," Issie nodded. "And that shouldn't be a problem for me."

"Good," Ginty said, and then stopped talking as Issie started getting undressed in the middle of the feed room! She stripped off her Dulmoth Park sweatshirt and held it out to Ginty.

"Sorry, it needs a wash," Issie said as she handed it over. "I slept in it this morning."

Ginty seemed puzzled. "Why are you giving me your uniform?"

"Because I won't need it any more..." Issie took a deep breath. "I quit."

Chapter 13

As they drove away from the stables, Mrs Brown cast a glance at her daughter sitting beside her. Issie had always been headstrong and impetuous. There were times when Mrs Brown worried about having a child with such a wilful nature, but at moments like this she was deeply proud. Issie always stood up for what she believed in – even if it meant losing the job of her dreams.

"Thanks for coming to get me, Mum," Issie said, "and for bringing me a clean sweatshirt. I'm sorry for all the drama."

"Well," Mrs Brown smiled at her, "I could hardly expect you to make your own way home in your pyjama top, could I?"

Issie's explanation for being at Dulmoth Park had been quite simple: Verity had surprised her very early that morning, calling by at the house. The two girls had come to the stables together and Issie had stayed behind to confront her boss. It was kind of the truth – minus the bits about Mystic, of course. Better than trying to explain that she'd ridden here in the middle of the night on her grey pony. Mystic had remained Issie's secret for so long now, she wouldn't have dreamt of telling anybody about him, not even her mum.

She'd told her mother all about Ginty, though. And when she phoned up from the stables and said she'd quit, Mrs Brown had come straight away to collect her. Now she reached out and took Issie's hand in her own and gave it a tight squeeze.

"Issie?"

"Yes, Mum?"

"Maybe next time it would be easier if you just took the job at the law firm?"

Issie began to giggle. "I know! My first proper job and I accuse my boss of doping the horses!"

Mrs Brown laughed. "Yes, well, admittedly it's not

going to look great on your CV. Still, I wish I'd seen the look on Ginty's face when you told her you were leaving."

"She had her mouth open like a goldfish," Issie said. "She couldn't believe it."

"So," Mrs Brown said, "where to now, my unemployed daughter? You must be exhausted. Do you want to go straight home?"

"No, Mum," Issie shook her head. "I've got one more stop I need to make on the way."

It was still early, not yet 7 a.m., as Issie and Mrs Brown pulled up outside Tom Avery's cottage at Winterflood Farm. Avery was awake, though – like most horsey people he tended to get up ridiculously early. By seven he had already fed his horses and was in the kitchen making a pot of tea when he heard the car pull up outside. He opened the front door to greet Issie and her mother before they had the chance to knock.

"Mrs B! Issie!" Avery smiled at them both warmly. If he was still upset about the conversation he'd had with Issie the last time she called round, he didn't show it. "Come inside. I've just made some tea." He led the way to the kitchen. "I must say I wasn't expecting company for breakfast. I don't usually get visitors at this hour." He smiled at Issie. "In fact, shouldn't you be at work right now?"

"Well, yes… and no…" Issie said. "The thing is, Tom, I've quit."

Mrs Brown interjected. "We've just come back from the stables. Issie gave Ginty what-for and told her she didn't want to work for her because she caught her putting capsicums on the horses."

Issie rolled her eyes. "Mum! Not capsicums! I caught her using *capsaicin*!"

"Capsaicin?" Avery's expression turned serious. "Are you sure?"

"Uh-huh," Issie nodded. "She's got a whole medicine chest of stuff that she's been using. Tottie's got terrible arthritis, but Ginty's been masking it by injecting her with loads of bute so they can keep jumping her for the rest of the season and then sell her."

"I take it that Tottie is worth a lot of money?" asked Avery.

Issie nodded. "Ginty doesn't even own her. She's one of Cassandra Steele's horses."

"I know Cassandra," Avery said. "She's one of the patrons of my Horse Welfare auxiliary. Cassandra's a good egg. I'd be very surprised if she knew that Ginty was doping her horses."

"I must say you don't look particularly shocked by any of this, Tom," Mrs Brown said.

"I'm not," Avery said bluntly. "I've suspected this sort of behaviour from Ginty for a long time now."

"So why didn't you warn Issie before she went to work there?" Mrs Brown demanded. "Do you realise what she's been through with this woman—"

"Mum! Stop!" Issie's voice was wobbly. "Tom did warn me. He told me that Ginty's methods were awful and he didn't want me to work for her. And I ignored him and did it anyway." Issie turned to Avery. "I'm really sorry, Tom. I should have listened to you. I thought I knew better than you, but I was wrong."

Avery shook his head. "You have nothing to apologise for. Ginty has fooled a lot of people in her time and not all of them wake up to her ways as quickly as you did. You had to make your own choices and learn from your own mistakes. So consider it forgotten, OK? Let's just put the whole debacle behind us."

Issie wasn't so sure. "I'm so worried about Flame, Tom. He's so sensitive and he's getting worse and now I've abandoned him too…"

Avery passed her a cup of tea. "Take a sip of this and calm yourself down," he said gently. "It's not over yet. I may still be able to do something about Flame."

"What do you mean?" Issie asked.

But Avery just smiled and said, "I told you to drink your tea! And leave Flame to me."

"But what can Avery possibly do? Flame is one of Ginty's horses and everyone knows that Ginty can't stand Tom! She's hardly going to hand Flame over to him!" Stella squawked when Issie told her the news that afternoon at the River Paddock.

It was the first time in ages that Issie had seen her two best friends. When she phoned Stella and Kate and asked them if they wanted to go for a hack, they had both seemed a little surprised. They were even more shocked when Issie met them at the paddock and filled them in on the whole story. It wasn't easy to finish because Stella kept interrupting to gasp "I knew it!" and "Ohmygod!" all the way through.

When she did finally get to the end, Issie had one more thing to tell them. "I'm sorry," she said, "Aidan was right. I've been acting like a stuck-up idiot for weeks now, ignoring my horses and my two best friends, and I didn't even realise it."

"Is that what he said to you?" Stella was horrified. "Issie, you might have been a stuck-up idiot, but you're our stuck-up idiot! Aidan can't speak to you like that. Just wait until I see him!"

"Ummm… thanks, I guess," Issie said, and the three girls giggled and hugged. "Welcome back, Issie. We missed you!" Kate said.

Issie's horses had missed her too. She had hardly had the chance to ride Blaze and Comet over the past few weeks and the skewbald pony was so fresh and full of energy when they went out hacking that day, Issie had trouble holding him back.

"You're back on a vigorous exercise schedule for the rest of the week to cool you down a bit!" she told Comet as the skewbald arrived back at the paddock still full of beans, jogging restlessly beneath her despite the two-hour hack she had given him along the riverbank past Winterflood Farm.

As they rode past Avery's house Issie had wanted to turn down the driveway and pop in to see him again and ask exactly what his plan was. When she had left his house that morning Avery seemed quite confident that he could help Flame. But what could Tom do when the horse was still stabled with Ginty?

For the rest of the week, Issie waited and tried desperately not to think about Flame. At least being unemployed meant that she could focus on her own horses once more. She spent nearly all her time down at the River Paddock with Blaze and Comet and, even though she certainly no longer rated Ginty as a trainer, she had to admit that she found she was riding better than she had done before she went to work at Dulmoth Park.

"I'm not surprised," Avery said when she told him this, "you've been riding a roster of at least six horses a day for almost a month. All those hours in the saddle must have built up your reflexes and muscle tone."

It was a Friday afternoon. Avery had called Issie up and they had been chatting on the phone for a bit when the instructor broke the big news. "It's all on for Saturday," he said. "Meet me at my house at seven tomorrow morning. Wear your best jods and your long boots and something smart like a nice shirt – we need to look professional."

"OK…" Issie said hesitantly, "but why? Where are we going? What's on?"

"I'll explain on the way to the horse show," Avery told her.

"Horse show?" Issie was confused. "What horse show? Tom?"

But it was too late. Avery had already hung up the phone.

Cleveland Valley was one of the poshest showgrounds on the outskirts of Chevalier Point. It was surrounded by giant oak trees and in the centre of the green fields, the arenas were marked out with white picket fences. Grandstands had been set up so that you could sit and watch the action in all three rings at once and never miss a thing.

There was also a well-equipped area with wash bays and horse pens where the competitors could park their horse trucks and floats.

Among the rows of trucks belonging to the various riders it was easy to spot Ginty McLintoch's. Her silver and gold truck stood out in the crowd. Ginty had arrived early that morning with Penny and Natasha and six of her best competition horses – including Tottie and Flame.

As she walked towards the sparkling horse truck, Issie wondered how Natasha was coping with Ginty. She hadn't dared to try and talk to Natasha on the morning that she left Dulmoth Park. She'd phoned Natasha at home and left a long, rambling message telling her what had happened, but she hadn't heard back. So Issie wasn't surprised when Natasha saw her coming and raced over to her. She didn't waste any time letting Issie know exactly what was on her mind.

"Maybe I'm stupid," Natasha said, "but I thought we'd actually become friends over the past few weeks, Issie."

"We are friends!" Issie said.

"So why did you leave like that without even saying goodbye?" Natasha pouted.

"I couldn't say anything – Ginty told me I had to pack my bags and get off the premises and besides, I didn't want her to see us together in case I got you into trouble too," Issie replied. "I didn't want her to think you were involved with me and Verity." She sighed. "Anyway, I told you all of this when I left the message on your phone! You were the one who never called me back!"

"What?" Natasha's face dropped. "What message? When?"

"The day that I left," Issie told her, "I phoned up and left a message on the answerphone at your house…" she paused as the truth dawned on her, "…and you probably never got it because your dad heard my voice so he deleted it! I bet he never told you that I called."

Natasha sighed. "That sounds about right. Dad really doesn't like you, Issie. Not after what happened with the golf club. He was furious when he found out you were working at Ginty's. He didn't want me hanging out with you…"

"I suppose I should have thought of that," Issie said. "I thought you'd got the message and you just didn't care about me leaving."

"Of course I cared!" Natasha said, sounding genuinely hurt. "It's been awful at those stables since you left. There's no one to talk to and I have to do all the work. Penny's such a suck-up she won't say a word against Ginty. She was the one who told me you had been fired because Ginty caught you stealing."

"What?" Issie was horrified. "I wasn't stealing! And I wasn't fired! I quit because I found out that Ginty has been doping the horses. Tottie is lame with arthritis and all this time Ginty's been keeping her competing by injecting her with bute. And that liniment she's using isn't—"

"Natasha!" Ginty's deep voice interrupted them. The two girls looked up, startled. The look on Ginty's face when she saw who Natasha was talking to was positively thunderous.

"What are you doing here, Isadora? I wasn't expecting you to show your face again." The trainer walked down the ramp of the horse truck to confront Issie. "I thought you'd be smart enough to stay away from my team and my horses," Ginty sneered. "You aren't welcome at my truck. Cassandra's going to be here any minute."

At that moment Issie caught sight of the millionairess. Cassandra was striding across the paddocks towards the truck, and walking beside her, chatting away and laughing as if they were old mates, was Tom Avery.

"Cassandra!" Ginty smiled warmly and strode forward to meet her. She gritted her teeth, "…and Tom. What a *pleasant* surprise to see you here!"

"Oh, don't talk rot, Ginty!" Cassandra said bluntly. "It's no secret that you and Tom don't get on. I might not indulge in much of the gossip that goes on around the show circuit, but even I know that much!"

Ginty's jaw dropped open.

"I'm here with some news," Cassandra continued, "Tom gave me a call earlier in the week and told me that he's got some space in his stable at the moment and that he'd really like to try his hand at a bit of training. When he asked whether I might be interested in moving Flame over to Winterflood Farm I gave the matter some thought and my answer was yes."

"You're kidding me!" Ginty said.

"I'm hardly likely to make jokes about my horses,

Ginty," Cassandra replied. "And you can't honestly be surprised by this. Your training hasn't exactly been aceing it in terms of results with Flame. He's been a disaster every time I've seen him. When Tom called me and said he'd like to do some schooling with Flame I found myself agreeing all too easily!"

"But we have a contract," Ginty spluttered. "I'm in charge of Flame's training… it's always been my plan to bring him on slowly."

"Oh, really?" Cassandra said. "You told me that he'd be ready to compete in the North Island Championships. That's just two weeks away, and this horse appears to be getting worse, not better."

"We've had some setbacks," Ginty stammered. "My… my head groom left and—"

"Oh, for goodness' sake, Ginty," Cassandra said dismissively, "I don't want excuses. I want results. Anyway, I don't see why you're so bothered. It's only one horse. You'll hardly miss him. I don't need to remind you that I have at least another twenty horses still stabled with you, so unless you want all of them to be moved immediately I don't think there should be any talk about my contractual obligations, do you? I've made up my mind. I'm giving Flame to Avery. Just to see what sort of a job he does with him. Perhaps I've had all my eggs in one basket for too long."

As Cassandra walked away from the horse truck, Ginty managed to keep a pleasant smile fixed on her face, but the moment the millionairess was out of sight, she rounded on Avery like a vicious pitbull.

"Very clever," she growled at Tom, "manouevring your way in like that with Cassandra, trying to ruin my business."

"I'm not doing this to spite you, Ginty," Avery replied coolly, "I'm doing this for the good of the horse. Not that I expect you to understand that concept."

"Well, good luck to you and your rebel riders!" Ginty snarled as she handed him Flame's lead rope. "You'll have your hands full with that can of pet food!"

"She's got a point," Issie said as she walked back with Avery, leading Flame to his horse truck. "Maybe we are out of our depth. Cassandra said she's expecting Flame to compete in two weeks at the North Island show, but it's impossible to have him ready in time. You haven't seen what Flame is like in the show ring. Last time he completely demolished half the jumps!"

"It's a tight deadline," Avery admitted, "but I wouldn't have agreed to it if I didn't think we could do it. This horse is the son of Brilliant Fire, Isadora. Look at his conformation – the strength in those haunches and hocks, the athletic slope of his shoulder. It's his birthright, it's in his blood. That amazing jump is inside him somewhere. All we need to do is convince him."

Beside them, Flame raised his head up high and looked around the showgrounds. His eyes widened and his nostrils flared as he let out a shrill whinny. It was a clarion call, the kind that a stallion makes when he is preparing to fight, and Issie suddenly found herself having to grip tightly to Flame's halter to hold on to the gelding.

"Easy, Flame," Issie said, trying to calm the big chestnut horse. "Not today, but soon, I promise. We'll come back and we'll show them what you can really do." She turned to her instructor. "When do we start?"

Avery smiled. "How about straight away?"

Chapter 14

All the way home, Avery questioned Issie about Flame. He insisted that Issie go into great detail describing the rapping sessions. He also wanted to know everything about the horse's care at Dulmoth Park – from the feed and tack that Ginty used to the studs that Flame wore in his shoes when he jumped.

"I don't see why you need to know all of this," Issie said at one point.

"If we're going to fix Flame, then I need to know what broke him in the first place," Avery said matter-of-factly.

By the time they had arrived at Winterflood Farm, Avery was fully briefed and ready to hit the ground running.

"Normally I'd give a new horse a day to settle and let him loose in the paddock to get used to the place," Avery told Issie as they unloaded Flame from the horse truck. "But time is a luxury we don't have. We need to get this horse working and thinking positively again straight away."

He handed Issie the lead rope. "Take him over to the first loose box in the stables and put on the old Pessoa jumping saddle that's in the tack room – it should fit him nicely."

"What about a bridle?" Issie asked. She had only just realised that they didn't have the Dutch gag. "We left all of Flame's gear with Ginty."

"It's all right," Avery said. "We won't be using the gag bit. You put on the saddle. I need to unearth a rather special piece of equipment that I haven't used for quite some time…"

Flame was intrigued by his new surroundings and held his head high, sniffing at the air, but he was reassured by the sound of Issie's voice and stood still as she tacked him up. She had the Pessoa saddle on Flame's back with the girth done up and was busy adjusting the stirrups to her length when Avery returned to the loose box. In his hands he held what looked like a bridle. But this wasn't like any bridle that Issie had seen before – there was no bit!

"Have you ever ridden in a hackamore?" Avery asked her. Issie looked at the strange contraption and shook her head. "What is it?"

"It's a bitless bridle," Avery reached up and slipped off Flame's halter and put the contraption over the horse's head.

Issie felt the knot of nerves in her tummy tighten as she watched Avery adjusting the noseband and the reins. "You mean there's no bit at all?" she asked. It was hard enough to stop Flame when he had the powerful Dutch gag in his mouth to hold him back – and now Avery was putting a bridle on the horse that seemed to be nothing more than reins and a noseband!

"I don't get how I'm supposed to keep him under control with nothing," Issie said. She was trying to trust Avery and not question his methods, but how could she believe that this was going to work?

Avery sensed her reluctance and tried to reassure her. "Don't be fooled by the lack of metal in the horse's mouth," he said. "Hackamores can be very powerful.

This one is a Blair Hackamore. It's the exact same bridle that I used in the showjumping ring on Starlight." Starlight was Avery's former world-class eventing mare. "She was a brilliant jumper in her day," he continued, "but so strong! She would almost wrench my arms out of their sockets... until I put her in this bridle."

He had finished doing up the hackamore and led Flame out into the arena next to the stables, with Issie walking by his side. "Gag bits are all well and good and some horses do need them, but it's not the solution for Flame's problem." Avery gave Issie a leg-up on to Flame's back. "It's no use getting into a tug of war with this horse, because he's much stronger than you. He could throw you across the arena with his head if he wanted to, so you have to convince him in other, smarter ways to do what you want."

Issie nodded. "So what do you want me to do?"

"Take a couple of laps to warm him up at a trot so he can get used to the feel of the hackamore," Avery told her, "and then I want you to ride him over this small fence here in the middle of the arena exactly the same way that you've been riding him over the jumps when you train with Ginty."

As she rode around the arena, Issie had to admit that the hackamore certainly seemed to exert control over the horse. She only needed to put the lightest pressure on the reins and Flame would slow down or halt. After a couple of laps, he was trotting quite nicely and Issie turned down the centre of the arena to face the jump.

As soon as Flame caught sight of the fence and realised what was about to happen, his attitude totally changed. He began to canter up and down on the spot, crab-stepping and holding his head high in the air just as he always did when he faced a jump at Ginty's.

With the hackamore on him, Issie was able to hold Flame back and keep him contained tightly, but she was wrestling with him until the last very minute when she could see the stride ahead of her. At that moment she suddenly dropped the reins, letting Flame go, and the horse shot forward like a skyrocket and flew the fence.

"Good boy, Flame!" Issie was smiling as she brought Flame back to Avery. But there was a dark frown on her instructor's face and he was anxiously raking his brown curly hair back off his face with both hands, as if something was bothering him intensely. Issie knew that things were very, very wrong.

"So this is how Ginty has been training you to jump him then?" Avery shook his head in disgust. "Well, it's worse than I thought. She's ruined a perfectly good horse and we're going to have to start right at the beginning."

Issie's face fell. She knew that Flame was behaving badly, but up until now she had been convinced that the problems could mostly be blamed on him. It was clear that Avery didn't see it that way at all.

"Let me ask you this," he said to Issie, "when you turn him round to face the jump and he begins to crab-step like that, what do you think is going through his head?"

Issie frowned. "I suppose he's over-excited? He's dying to jump..."

Avery groaned. "Showjumping riders often say that their horses *love to jump*. They think that's why their mounts pull like mad, canter on the spot and charge at the fences." Avery shook his head. "These are not signs that the horse is happy to jump. Quite the opposite. The horse is stressed. The reason he begins to pull and canter sideways like a crab is because he's having a panic attack about what is to come. And you're the one that's causing it!"

"Me?" Issie was taken aback. "What am I doing?"

"Holding him back like a cork in a champagne bottle that's ready to pop!" Avery said. "I know, I know, that's the way that Ginty has trained you to jump him. That's how all her riders do it, holding their horse back until they can 'see the stride'. It's disastrous and it makes the horses panic."

Issie thought back to her first day at Ginty's stables. Avery was right. She had never ridden like that before with tightened reins, holding the horse back, until Ginty had forced her to do it. She had become accustomed to Ginty's techniques – even though she knew all along in her heart that they were wrong.

"So how do we fix it?" she asked.

"We go right back to the beginning," Avery said. He walked over towards the jump in the middle of the arena that Issie had just taken Flame over a moment before and began dismantling it, taking away the poles and the jump stands. "We have to unlearn his panic behaviour."

"Unlearn?"

"That's right," Avery smiled at her. "Flame needs basic retraining to erase all that nonsense that Ginty has put into his head."

Avery had been lugging away the posts and rails of the showjump piece by piece as he spoke. He finally moved the last jump stand away from the middle of the arena so that there was nothing left except a single painted pole lying on the ground.

Avery rolled the pole and arranged it into position. "Get him settled into a rhythmic, active trot and then when he's ready, bring him over the pole."

"A pole?" Issie screwed up her face. "You want me to trot him over a pole?"

"What's the problem?" Avery asked sarcastically. "Do you think it's a bit much for you to handle?"

"Tom!" Issie argued. "In two weeks' time I'm going to be riding Flame at the North Island show. The jumps are going to be a metre twenty! I don't see what good trotting over a lousy pole is supposed to do."

"I tell you what," Avery replied, "if you can you trot him perfectly over the pole with no fuss and no rushing, I'll raise the bar immediately to one metre twenty. OK?"

"Sure," Issie agreed. This was ridiculous! Flame could trot over the pole easily!

As it turned out, the pole was far more of a challenge than Issie ever thought it would be. The very first time she turned Flame to face it he completely freaked, tried to charge at the pole and leapt about a metre high over it as if he were jumping in the World Cup! It took Issie a whole lap of the arena to settle him down again afterwards.

"You see?" Avery said. "It's not the size of the fence that rattles him. It's the very idea of jumping. It's like the chicken and the egg. He panics because he's held back, and he's held back because he's panicking." Avery looked at Flame's legs. "Ginty would have made the situation worse when she started using the capsaicin. For horses who are confident, established jumpers, capsaicin might encourage them to pick up their feet a little more carefully. But for a horse like Flame who is green and terrified by the whole prospect of jumping, putting capsaicin on his legs is utterly cruel. He associates painted poles with pain. Just the sight of them makes him scared."

Issie nodded. "OK, so you're right. It's back to square one. So what do we do now?"

"The next time you approach the pole, I want you to keep Flame on a loose rein. In fact, hold the rein all the way back at the buckle. Do you think you can do that?"

Issie boggled at this. "I don't think so. He's going to bolt."

Avery disagreed. "He won't bolt. If you keep your body position entirely still and don't change a single thing then he should stay calm. Try it."

As Issie rode Flame at a trot around the arena, she focused hard on doing nothing at all, staying perfectly still and letting the chestnut gelding relax on a loose rein. As soon as she turned to face the jump, though, Flame began to speed up.

"Stay perfectly still! Don't change your position!" Avery shouted at her. But it was too late. Flame was already in a mad gallop heading for the pole on the ground and Issie was snatching back her reins.

"I told you to stay still!" Avery shouted afterwards.

"I did stay still!" Issie yelled back.

"You moved," Avery said. "You leant forward and you snatched at the reins. Try it again, but this time, do it at a walk."

Issie couldn't believe she had been reduced to this. Flame was supposed to be a world-class jumper, and her training instruction was to make him walk over a pole on the ground! But she could understand Avery's methods now. They would not be raising the rail to one metre twenty today. Instead, she would have to take things slow with this horse. Flame had to unlearn all the problems that Ginty had created.

"Steady, Flame," she cooed to the big chestnut as she walked him back towards the pole on the ground. She was trying to keep her position utterly immobile as she asked him to keep his rhythm and step over the pole without a fuss. This time, Flame relaxed, kept a steady stride and stepped over the pole. Success! Issie was suddenly quite pleased with herself – even though all she'd done was walk over a pole!

"And now come through once more, this time at a trot," Avery instructed.

Issie asked Flame to trot on, and this time she had the reins loose and her hands all the way back at the buckle as the horse approached the pole. At the last minute, though, Flame speeded up and bolted the jump again!

"You flinched," was Avery's assessment as Issie brought the horse back to try once more. "This time, keep your hands at the buckle and do not move your body in the saddle at all. Just let him keep trotting as if the jump isn't there. Don't look for a stride, let the fence come to you."

It was hard to keep still and not flinch Issie realised, especially when you expect your horse to bolt at any moment. But she did as Avery said, steeling her nerve and keeping in the same position, her reins loose as she rode at the pole. This time as Flame turned to confront the pole, he remained at a calm trot – no mad gallops or wild crab-steps. They had done it! Flame was behaving like a normal horse!

"Well done, boy!" Issie was beaming as she gave him a slappy pat on his glossy neck.

"Yes, very good. I think that's enough for today," Avery said. "You can get off him now. Go untack him and give him his feed."

"You're kidding!" Issie said. "That's it?"

"I'm quite serious," Avery responded. "We've just ended our lesson on a good note."

"But we're hardly going to win the North Island show by trotting over a pole!"

"Better trotting over it than crashing into it," Avery said wryly. "Come on, let's settle him into his stall and then you can give him a good grooming."

For the rest of the week, the jump stands continued to remain dormant on the side of the arena as Avery's training sessions involved nothing more than poles lying on the ground.

At first, Flame would start every lesson back at square one. His ingrained instincts from those days at Ginty's stables were so strong that he'd take one look at the poles before panicking and trying to rush them. Avery would instruct Issie to sit back and relax, and keep her reins loose. It wasn't easy letting the reins loose on a mad horse who wanted to bolt, but Issie would do as he said and once Flame understood that the poles were nothing to get worked up over, he would settle down until pretty soon they were trotting around the arena in a steady rhythm.

By Friday, they were cantering the poles and Issie was thrilled when Flame kept a lovely regular pace around the arena.

"He's made excellent progress," Avery said as they led him back to the stables that evening.

"Yeah," Issie said, unable to keep her sarcasm in check, "if there's a competition at the North Island show for jumping over poles on the ground then we'll totally ace it."

Avery sighed. "I thought I'd explained it to you already, Issie. It's not about the size of the jump. It's about developing the horse's mind so that he feels secure in the arena."

"How do we know how he'll feel when the jumps do get to a proper size, though?" Issie asked.

"Let's find out," Avery said. "We'll take Flame to the pony-club rally with us tomorrow."

Stella and Kate were both at the pony-club rally that day, and when Issie told them about Avery's training, and how she'd spent the past week trotting over poles on the ground, they couldn't stop laughing.

"I'm sorry, Issie," Stella said wiping her eyes, "but it just seems like a bit of a come-down, doesn't it? One minute you're off at a professional stable jumping over huge fences and the next you're at Avery's house again trotting over poles like being back at kindergarten!"

Issie took their laughter with good humour. She didn't even mind when Stella and Kate told Dan and Ben about her trotting pole sessions and they joined in on the joke. Dan even laid his whip down on the ground and dared Issie to leap over it. "If it's not too high for you," he added before bursting into fits of giggles.

Things got more serious, however, when the senior ride headed up to the jumping arena after lunch. Avery set the fences at one metre. It was a short course, but there were some tricky combinations, including a double with a bounce stride in between the jumps and a very wide oxer to finish. As Dan, Ben, Stella and Kate all took their turns around the course, Issie sat and watched. When it was her turn, Avery called her over for a few last-minute words of advice.

"How does Flame feel?" Avery asked.

"He's been great all morning," Issie said. "He was lovely to ride with the other horses in the dressage training. He's been a superstar so far."

"Excellent," Avery agreed. "Now here is what I want you to do, Issie. I want you to take him into the showjumping ring, and ride him around the same course that the others have just done. Keep him at a steady working canter…" Avery looked at her, "…but don't go over any of the jumps."

"What?" Issie was confused. "What do you mean?"

"Just ride around in between and near the fences, to make him think he's going to be jumping. But don't actually jump. Give him a steady canter around for a couple of rounds and then we'll finish up for the day."

"You mean he's not going to jump at all?" Issie groaned. "Ohmygod, Tom! This is worse than the poles on the ground!"

"Issie, today is a vital part of Flame's rehabilitation," Avery said. "You need to think about the jumps here at the pony club as nothing more than an extension of his lessons at home. It's all part of the training, Issie. Even the competitions are nothing more than fancy schooling sessions with prizes. Don't ever lose sight of that."

Issie seemed to accept this, but she still had a question. "How is he ever going to learn to jump if I never do any jumping?"

"Flame already knows how to jump," Avery told her. "What he needs to learn is how to control his stress, to stay calm when he's confronted with jumps. I want him to canter around that show ring without having to jump a thing, so he can figure out for himself that there's nothing scary about showjumps."

Issie looked over at Stella, Kate, Dan and Ben sitting

on their ponies on the sideline waiting to watch her take her turn.

"Taking big jumps might impress your friends," Avery agreed, "but that's not what Flame needs."

Issie nodded. "I understand, Tom." She smiled. "We're ready to do our round now."

Flame cantered around the jumps beautifully and Issie concentrated on staying steady and still in two-point position as she rode past the jumps without taking a single one of them. She had to laugh as she left the arena that day and saw the puzzled expressions on her friends' faces.

"Well," Dan teased, "I suppose technically you just got a clear round in there. You didn't stop and you didn't knock down a single rail."

Avery, however, was genuinely happy with her progress. "Nice round," the instructor told her. "He went perfectly."

Issie had hoped that Avery's praise for Flame's performance at the pony-club rally would translate to some actual jumps when they were back at Winterflood Farm the next day. But no. Once again, Avery asked her to school the big chestnut over poles on the ground. It was the same on Monday, Tuesday, Wednesday, Thursday and Friday. The North Island show was on Sunday and by Saturday Issie couldn't control the urge any longer. She finally asked Avery if there was any chance at all that they might actually be doing some real jumps at training today.

"Oh," Avery replied airily, "I don't think we want to overface him the day before the big show, do you?" He smiled at Issie. "Just take him for a gentle hack today. No point in being in the arena – he's learnt everything he needs to know."

"You can't be serious!" Issie was stunned. "We're competing tomorrow! We haven't jumped a single jump."

"I'm totally serious," Avery replied. "You and Flame are ready to win. And tomorrow – you're going to prove it."

Chapter 15

Flame looked every inch a champion when Issie unloaded him from the horse truck on the morning of the North Island Championships. With his mane plaited and his coat buffed to a deep copper shine the chestnut gelding certainly had an air of winning glamour about him.

The horse looked brilliant, but it was what was underneath the surface that had Issie worried. Flame was still unproven. In the past two weeks under Avery's tuition Flame hadn't jumped a single fence. Issie couldn't help but be concerned that their reschooling efforts so far had amounted to nothing more than poles on the ground. Hardly adequate preparation for the level of competition they would encounter at the showgrounds today!

Issie felt the knot of nerves in her tummy tighten as she looked over at the main arena. Avery had entered Flame in the one metre qualifier class. This was the final chance for Flame to be graded and continue in the competitions this season. More importantly than that, however, Cassandra Steele would be in the stands. Avery had spoken to Flame's owner on the phone last night and she had made it quite clear that she would be watching them today to assess his progress.

"Nervous?" Avery asked as he emerged from the horse truck.

"A little," Issie had to admit.

"Don't be," Avery said firmly. "Flame went brilliantly at the rally the other day. He's ready for this."

Issie boggled at Avery's confidence. "Tom! All he did at pony club was canter around a bit! We didn't jump a single fence, and those fences out there are a metre high!"

Avery brushed aside Issie's concerns. "He'll be fine. Just get him nicely balanced, responsive and calm, and trust me, the jumping won't be an issue."

Issie shook her head in disbelief, but it was clear that

there was no point in arguing. She had to have faith that Avery knew what he was doing. And so she continued to groom the horse while Avery busied himself doing up the buckles on Flame's tendon boots and pulling on his bellboots.

"That's a lot of bandaging you're doing," Issie observed as she watched Avery move on to the hind legs and use gamgee and gauze to wrap the tendons at the back.

"Flame needs protection on his legs," Avery said. "We don't want him getting spooked if he bangs a rail."

As Avery finished the leg bandages, Issie tightened the girth one more hole on the Pessoa saddle. "Shall I put the hackamore on now?" she asked.

Avery shook his head. "Leave the halter on for now and give him a hay net to keep him occupied while we walk the course," he told her. "We've got ages before the competition begins."

It was busy in the arena during the course-walk session. There were around twenty riders in Issie's class that day, and most of them were in the arena checking out the jumps and learning the course off by heart.

Issie loved walking a jumping course with Avery. She was amazed at the difference it made to see the jumps through his eyes. This time, Avery particularly focused on a combination fence with two elements that he clearly thought would cause problems for the competitors.

"You must make sure you come in with a very straight line right down the centre and push on hard in order to get two strides in..."

"Well," a voice behind them said, "I must say it's nice to see you two back together again!"

Issie turned around to see Araminta, Aidan and Morgan, all dressed in their competition shirts and their best white jods.

Araminta smiled. "You know, everyone on the circuit is gossiping about it. I hear that Cassandra Steele handed over one of her best horses to you, Tom. I'll bet Ginty's absolutely fuming!" Araminta looked amused by this. It was pretty clear that she wasn't a member of the Ginty McLintoch fan club either.

Standing next to Araminta, Aidan looked distinctly uncomfortable. While Araminta and Avery were talking he sidled over to Issie and whispered to her. "Can I talk to you for a moment? Alone?"

They walked away from the others, but riders kept jostling past them. The middle of a showjumping ring wasn't exactly the most private place to have a deep and meaningful conversation. "Maybe we should talk later?" Issie said.

"No, I've something to say and it can't wait," Aidan replied. "I feel awful about our fight, and the things I said to you the other day... I want to say that I'm—"

"No!" Issie said to him. "Don't you dare tell me you're sorry. You were right, Aidan. I was being a bad friend – not just to Stella and Kate, but to you too. I made a big mistake trusting Ginty, but I want you to know that I've sorted it out now. Things are back to normal again."

"I can see that," Aidan smiled. "I just wanted to let you know that no matter what happens, I'm always there for you, OK?"

Issie smiled. "Thanks."

"Issie!" Avery shouted out to her. "Stop dawdling. We've got a course to walk! There'll be time to chat to your boyfriend later!"

Mortified with embarrassment, Issie blushed. "I don't

think that you're my boyfriend," she told Aidan. "I don't know why Tom said that."

Aidan gave her one of his killer smiles. "Well, I guess I was your boyfriend once upon a time. And I suppose... I could be again. That is, if you wanted me to be."

Issie felt her heart beating like mad. "Aidan, please... not now. I can't think about whether I want to be your girlfriend today. Not with the competition and everything that's going on..."

"I know," Aidan nodded. "We'll talk later, OK? Maybe go for a ride together?"

Issie smiled. "That would be really great."

As she walked back to the horse truck with Avery, Issie felt like a huge weight had been lifted off her shoulders. Now that she and Aidan were friends again, Issie could totally focus on the competition ahead of her. For the first time she actually found herself starting to feel excited at the prospect of riding Flame. It was less than an hour to the first event. As they were walking past the main arena, though, she had a moment of doubt when she caught sight of the familiar silver and gold logo of the Dulmoth Park horse truck.

"Ginty's here," Issie said. "She's parked just over there by the main arena."

"I know," Avery said with an unconcerned air. "I saw the truck when she arrived. The good news is it looks like she's only got two horses here today – Tokyo and Tottie. And neither of them will be entered against you – they're both in the next class."

However, Avery's confident demeanour didn't last. He returned from the judges' tent a few minutes later holding a piece of paper, positively fuming.

"That woman is a serpent! I can't believe she'd stoop to this!" Avery ranted.

"What's wrong?" Issie asked.

"Take a look at the running order for the first event of the day," Avery said, thrusting the piece of paper at Issie. "There are a few surprises."

Issie looked at the list and scanned down for her name to see where she was in the running order. She found it almost at the end, but directly above was another name that she hadn't been expecting to see.

"Natasha?" Issie was confused. According to the list Natasha Tucker was also riding in the one metre qualifier class – on Tottenham Hotspur!

"But Tottie shouldn't even be in my class!" Issie said. "She's been jumping over a metre twenty all season!"

Avery groaned. "I'm afraid Tottie still qualifies for the one metre class, so Ginty has every right to drop her down to compete in your ring."

"But that's not fair! Tottie's far too good."

"Ginty knows the rules and she knows the loopholes too. She knew that we'd be riding in the one metre class today. She's done this on purpose so she can beat us and crow about it in front of Cassandra."

Issie looked at the list of riders. "Natasha is riding just before me."

Knowing that she was competing against Natasha gave Issie an awful sinking feeling. She had thought that their love-hate relationship was finally sorted out. No more silly rivalries. Had she been wrong? Did Natasha know she'd be up against Issie today and all that stuff about being friends was just part of her game?

Avery sighed. "We can't afford to worry about Ginty's dirty tactics. You have to keep your mind on Flame. We need to convince him that this is nothing more than another rally day at the pony club."

Flame, however, already seemed to realise that this

wasn't the case. He had seen the horses warming up around him and he could smell the tension in the air. As Avery held the big chestnut ready for Issie to mount up, Flame raised his head high and gave a loud whinny. His blood was up and Issie could sense his excitement.

"He's OK," Avery insisted as Flame began to crab-step, jogging around like a racehorse while Avery clung on to the reins. "Keep him on a loose rein and walk him about to calm him down. He's a little hot, but that's to be expected. As long as you can stay calm, he'll be fine. He'll pick up on your energy. It's up to you to keep your cool."

"Shall I take him over the practice jump?" Issie asked.

Avery shook his head. "Not yet. There's plenty of time. Let's settle him in with some walking and trot work first, try and get a rhythm going."

With Avery instructing her, Issie spent the next twenty minutes working Flame in. He had such beautiful floating movement. Issie could feel the quality of his bloodlines expressed in every step. His quality showed through in his paces and his attitude and she could already feel the change in Flame as he responded to her now without fear or tension. Under Avery's guidance they had made so much progress in the past two weeks. And there was so much more still to do! When Issie caught sight of Cassandra Steele standing on the sidelines watching the ring, she suddenly realised that if the millionairess didn't like what she saw today then she'd take Flame away from Avery and he'd be returned to Ginty's stables. All the hard work they'd done to reschool the horse would be undone by Ginty's awful methods. Issie couldn't stand the thought of losing Flame like that. He had such a fantastic personality and he was trying so hard for her! She owed it to him to go into the arena and win.

"He's looking good, Issie." Avery's voice shook her back to reality. "I think he's ready. Ride him back to the truck and grab your showing jacket. I'm going to walk over to the practice fence, so meet me there."

At the horse truck Issie tied Flame to his hitching hook and unlocked the main door, climbing into the back of the truck. Her jacket was in the closet next to the tack box. She had packed it in a drycleaning bag to keep it safe. As she unzipped the bag and slipped it on, she felt a tingle of excitement. *I need to keep calm*, she told herself, *act like it's an ordinary day at the pony club, and Flame will stay relaxed...*

She took a deep breath and buttoned up the jacket, pausing for a moment to glance at her reflection in the mirrored door of the truck before she stepped outside once more. Flame was standing there waiting for her, but there was someone else beside him.

"Natasha?" Issie could see that she was in floods of tears. "Ohmygod! What's the matter?"

"It's Ginty!" Natasha sobbed. "She just fired me!"

"What?" Issie couldn't believe it. "How? Why?"

"I was getting Tottie ready for the event," Natasha sniffled, "and everything was fine until Ginty came over with this injection she wanted to give her. So I asked her, 'Is it bute?' and anyway she just went bonkers at me and said she was tired of being questioned by know-it-all grooms. Then she said I had to prove myself as a professional rider. And she gave me the needle and told me to inject Tottie."

Issie was appalled. "Did you do it?"

"Of course not! I told Ginty that bute is illegal

when you're competing, but then she told me that she wasn't interested in hearing my opinions and I didn't know anything... and well, I lost my temper at that point and said a few things... and she fired me!"

"But if she fired you," Issie said, "then who is riding Tottie?"

Her question was answered by the announcer's voice over the Tannoy. "There has been a change to the next combination in the arena today," the announcer said. "Instead of Natasha Tucker, Tottenham Hotspur will be ridden in this class by Penny Greville."

"Typical," Natasha said darkly. "I should have known Penny would take the ride. She's too much of a coward to stand up to Ginty."

The girls both turned their attention to the arena where Penny and Tottie were about to ride through the flags to take the first jump. Despite having just been assigned the last-minute ride on the dapple-grey mare, it seemed entirely likely that Penny would get a clear round. She had ridden Tottie many times before so she knew how to handle the mare. As for Tottie, the jumps were kindergarten stuff as far as she was concerned.

Sure enough, the jumps seemed a piece of cake for

the duo. Tottie rattled a couple of rails as she took the double, but nothing fell. "She's going to go clear," Natasha said through gritted teeth as she watched Tottie clear the sixth fence and then pop neatly over fence number seven.

Tottie was on her way to take fence number eight when Issie heard Aidan shouting out her name. He was cantering Fortune over and waving frantically at Issie as if something was wrong.

"What are you two doing?" Aidan asked as he pulled up beside them. "Natasha? Shouldn't you be in that ring now?"

"Penny is riding Tottie instead," Issie explained.

"Ginty fired me!" Natasha said.

"She's totally crazy," Aidan sympathised before turning his attention to Issie. "Tom sent me to find you. He's been looking for you everywhere! He's been waiting for you at the practice jump."

"Ohmygod!" Issie gasped. She was due in the ring straight after Natasha – only Natasha wasn't riding any more. Penny was! Which meant it was her turn next!

As she raced toward the practice fence, Issie's heart was pounding. She could see Tom standing there waiting for her, looking tense as he checked his watch.

"There you are!" he cried out with relief when he saw her. "Where have you been? We're totally out of time."

"It's OK," Issie insisted. "We've still got a couple of minutes. They haven't called my name yet—"

Suddenly the loudspeaker crackled to life. "Isadora Brown, riding Flame. Proceed now to arena number one."

"Ohmygod!" Issie was struck with panic.

"It's OK, Issie," Avery said, as he gave her a leg-up. "The main thing is to keep your cool. We're out of time, but Flame is already warmed up. You don't need a practice jump – he'll be fine. Off you go!"

"I still have a minute before I have to be in the ring," Issie pleaded. "There's enough time, Tom. Let me do one jump!"

"Issie, there's not enough time. If you rush him—" Avery began to say. But Issie wasn't listening. She urged the big chestnut into a trot and circled him towards the practice jump. She took just a moment to eye up the cross rails, getting the practice fence in her sights. Her palms were wet with sweat. How much time did she have? It must be less than a minute by now. Was that enough time to get over the jump and then into the arena and through the flags? Beneath her she felt Flame tense up as she turned him to face the jump. The horse could sense the sudden urgency in his rider. He shook his head, trying to release himself from the hackamore restraining him, and without even thinking about it, Issie fought back.

"Have patience," Avery called out to her. "Stop trying to look for the stride. Let the jump come to you."

But Issie still wasn't listening. Her hands gripped tighter on the reins as the gelding fought her even more and then suddenly it was just like the old days at Ginty's stables – Flame racing at the fence with his head in the air and Issie hauling on the reins.

In front of the jump Issie threw the reins at him and Flame took two massive strides as if he were readying himself to leap but then, at the last minute, he changed his mind and skidded into the jump.

Issie felt the horse pull up and went into a defensive position, throwing her weight back and doing her best to hang on as Flame ploughed straight into the rails, crashing into them hard with his chest and scattering them everywhere!

It had all gone horribly wrong. Flame had refused to jump and had bowled the whole fence over instead!

"Isadora Brown on Flame – this is your last call. Into the arena now, please!" The voice over the loudspeaker was firm and clear. She had to go into the arena now or she would be disqualified!

There was no time left for Issie to attempt the practice jump again. With a sick feeling in her belly, jangled nerves and a leaden heart, she turned Flame away from the disastrous practice fence and rode the big chestnut into the arena to begin their round.

Chapter 16

Issie desperately needed a moment to settle Flame down – but the clock was ticking. She had run out of time and if she wanted to avoid being disqualified she had to cross the start line right now!

As she turned Flame towards the flags, the headstrong chestnut began to canter on the spot in anticipation. Their crash just moments before had really rattled his nerves. Issie could sense the tension bubbling under the surface, and she caught a glimpse of Flame's wild eyes, and the froth of sweat that had already formed on his neck. Flame was on a hair trigger, ready to go totally berserk!

Trying to keep control, Issie tightened her grip on

the reins. But it was like trying to hold back an elephant. Flame ignored her hands, surging forward and bolting at the first jump in a mad panic. Issie had no choice but to try and stay onboard as Flame leapt from too far out and bashed the top rail as he flew the fence, whacking it hard with both hind legs.

"Stop it, Flame!" Issie shouted angrily at him as she tried to wrestle the gelding back under control. The top rail had fallen, but really they were lucky they hadn't bowled the whole jump over!

At that moment Issie felt as if they were back in one of Ginty's awful training sessions. She had a vision of Flame losing control and mowing down everything in his path. It was as if all the hard work that she had done with Avery had never happened.

On the sidelines, Avery had his eyes glued on Issie and the big chestnut. They had come so far in the past two weeks, but now, in her hurry to get into the arena, Issie and Flame had fallen apart. The question was, could she pull the horse – and herself – back together again?

"Come on, Issie," Avery muttered under his breath. "Stop fighting him and start riding as a team."

In the arena, Issie was trying to unravel everything

that had gone wrong. Avery was right, of course. She should never have rushed the practice jump. Her panic had got Flame hyped-up when she should have been calming him down. It was all her fault. But it wasn't too late to fix her mistake. She had spent the past two weeks reschooling this horse with Avery. Surely there must be a way to settle Flame back down again?

With the next fence still a few strides away, Flame was bouncing up and down on the spot like a jack-in-the-box, fighting her every single step of the way.

"Flame, easy, boy, easy," Issie breathed softly to the horse. There was nothing else for it. The fighting and the tension had to stop.

Issie took a deep breath, sat heavy in the saddle and centered herself. She imagined that she wasn't even in a showjumping ring any more. She was at home at Winterflood Farm with Tom. This wasn't a competition – this was training. She remembered Avery's words. *It's all part of the training. Even the competitions are nothing more than fancy schooling sessions with prizes.*

Staying calm and focused, she checked the powerful Hanoverian, and this time he didn't fight her. Flame came to a complete halt.

On the sidelines, Aidan was completely baffled. Issie had suddenly stopped dead after the first jump. "What is she doing in there?"

"Issie's doing the right thing," Avery countered. "She's getting control back before she continues."

In the arena, Issie was talking softly to Flame. "Good boy." She gave him a reassuring pat on the neck. "It's no big deal. They're just little jumps. In fact, they're so little we're going to trot them!"

Keeping a light contact on the reins Issie asked Flame to trot on. She approached the second jump as if it were one of the poles on the ground in her schooling sessions back home, focusing on keeping a steady rhythm and letting Flame have his head, sliding the reins loose to the buckle.

"She's trotting!" Aidan was beside himself. "She'll never make it inside the time if she trots him!"

Avery disagreed. "She's doing brilliantly. It doesn't matter if they make the time."

Issie and Flame took two more fences at a trot. Each time, Issie kept totally still and calm, remembering Avery's words, trying to be patient and waiting for the jump to come to her.

When Flame took the fourth fence without rushing at all, Issie knew he was ready to canter. By now, she was oblivious to the crowds watching them. She was no longer concentrating on winning. She was a professional rider in training mode.

Flame cantered on and popped the next two fences as if they weren't even there. Issie kept him balanced between jumps by sitting back in the saddle to slow his stride. There was the odd moment when she felt the desperate urge to check him with a sharp pull as he came in a little fast or too close to a jump, but she always resisted it. She knew that Flame needed to learn to gauge his own take-off point, and the horse amazed her every time by rounding up and getting himself out of trouble. As they took the final jump and cantered back through the flags, they had only four faults on the board!

In the end, it wasn't the fastest round of the day. The trotting and the fussing had added extra seconds and taken a toll on the scoreboard. Issie and Flame finished up with three time faults along with the four jumping faults. That made seven faults in total. It wasn't a winning score, but for Flame it was a triumph. As they left the arena to the sound of raucous applause from Aidan, Avery and Natasha, Issie realised she had never been so pleased with a horse in all her life.

"Wasn't he great?" Issie was beaming as she rode out of the arena to meet them. "You were right, Tom. He jumped like a champion!"

"Fantastic!" Avery agreed. "You rode him perfectly."

"All he needs is a few more events like this one to get his confidence up," Issie said as she slid down off Flame's back. "I just need a bit more time and he'll be amazing."

She looked imploringly at Avery. "Tom, you have to convince Cassandra somehow. She has to understand that Flame is complicated. You couldn't expect him to win today after all he'd been through. She has to let us keep on training him!"

"I agree with you, Issie, but I don't know if Cassandra can be convinced," Avery said. "She was expecting results today, but there's no way we'll be in with a chance for a ribbon."

A few moments later, the final scores had been tallied. Issie and Flame had done better than she could have hoped. As expected, their seven faults wasn't good enough to win a ribbon, but it did put them in fourth place. At the top of the rankings of course, with a clear round and a super-quick time, were Penny and Tottie. Ginty had done exactly what she set out to do – beaten them hands-down in front of Cassandra.

Compared to Ginty's win, would Flame and Issie's fourth place be enough to keep Flame's owner happy? If Cassandra decided to take him back to Dulmoth Park then Issie couldn't stop her. She'd have no option but to let him go.

"What is taking them so long?" Avery looked at his watch. "They should have done the prize-giving for this class ten minutes ago! They're keeping everyone waiting now. The whole event will end up running behind schedule."

As if on Avery's command, the loudspeaker once again crackled back to life. "Ladies and gentlemen, we apologise for the delay. Could Cassandra Steele please come to the judges' tent immediately? Cassandra Steele, please come to the judges' tent now!"

"I don't get it…" Aidan looked at the empty arena. "Why aren't they announcing the winners?"

There was a look on Avery's face as if the penny had

suddenly dropped. He turned his gaze to the judges' tent, where a crowd seemed to be gathering.

"Come on!" Avery said. "The judges' tent! There's something happening!" And he strode off across the field towards the tent with Issie, Natasha and Aidan following closely behind him.

There was an angry crowd gathering at the tent. The competition was now officially running twenty minutes late and frustrated riders had begun to assemble, all of them trying to find out what was going on.

"Can everybody, please calm down!" A man in a suit was standing on a table just outside the tent addressing the riders. "We apologise for the delay. If you are entered in the next event we will be getting underway shortly. It appears there has been a problem with the previous event and an announcement is about to be made. The next event will start very shortly!"

"Excuse me." Avery tapped the shoulder of a woman standing in front of him. "Do you know what's going on?"

"Well," the woman said, "it seems that the horse that just won the last class was given a random drug test and failed it!"

"A random drug test?" Issie was stunned.

Avery nodded. "They often send the vet along to do them at the regional competitions."

"What would they test for?" asked Issie.

"Substances that are illegal in competitions," Avery said, "like bute or capsaicin."

"Ohmygod!" Issie gasped. "Tottie will be full of bute!"

Two seconds later the news crackled out for everyone to hear over the Tannoy. "We regret to announce that in the last class Penny Greville on Tottenham Hotspur has been disqualified. Would the following riders please now present themselves in the arena for prize giving: in first place, Veronica Perkins on Jupiter Jones, second is Chelsea Dunstan on Cleopatra, and third is Isadora Brown on Flame. Please come to the arena immediately to collect your ribbons. We apologise again for the delay."

Issie couldn't believe it. They had come third! Flame had won a ribbon.

"Don't dawdle," Avery said as he legged her up on to Flame's back. "They might give that ribbon to someone else!"

It was the longest prize giving Issie ever had to sit through. Not that she was ungrateful to get her ribbon

– she was beyond thrilled. But she was also desperate to get back over to the judges' tent and find out once and for all what had really gone on. As soon as she was out of the prize-giving ring, Natasha came bounding up to her, full of news.

"It was a random drug test!" She was panting and trying to catch her breath as she spoke. "Ginty was totally furious when the vet told her Tottie had tested positive. She hit the roof – but there was nothing she could do about it. You should see the stuff the vet's got in his kit. They've got these amazing scanners and all he had to do was run them over Tottie's legs and they could see that Ginty had used capsaicin on her!"

"So why did it take them so long?" Issie said.

"They had to do a proper blood test before they could disqualify her," Natasha continued. "They called Cassandra over because Tottie's her horse and of course Ginty denied everything – but then I showed the vet where the medicine locker was under the sink in the horse truck and that was it! As soon as they saw the capsaicin they disqualified her on the spot!"

"Ohmygod, Natasha! Ginty will totally kill you."

Natasha rolled her eyes. "Who cares! She's already

fired me. What else can she do? Anyway I was already going to move Romeo to a new stable. I'm fed up with Ginty's place. I'd like to keep him somewhere nice next time."

She smiled at Issie. "Do you think Avery has any room at Winterflood Farm?"

It turned out that Natasha wasn't the only one interested in talking to Avery. Cassandra Steele had a business proposition for him.

"Avery! I'm sure you've heard about the scandal?" Cassandra's sharp tone was even more dramatic than usual. "Clearly you and I have much to discuss. Things will have to change after the developments today. I must do what's best for my horses."

"Absolutely, Cassandra," Avery said. "We'd love to keep training Flame at Winterflood Farm if that's what you want."

"Good gravy, man!" Cassandra shook her head in bewilderment. "Are you barking? Of course you're keeping Flame! It's the others I'm worried about."

"I'm sorry?" Avery was confused. "What others?"

"All my horses!" Cassandra said. "I've fired Ginty. I've given her the rest of the day to pack her bags and get off the premises. I've already sent security guards to accompany her while she picks up her things. They'll escort her from the grounds and change the codes on the gate so she can't get back in again."

Cassandra pulled herself up to her full height – which wasn't very high at all – and looked Avery in the eye.

"With Ginty gone, I've got a stable full of world-class horses that need looking after. And that's where you come in. I'd like to make you an offer, Tom."

Cassandra Steele smiled. "I'd like you to take over at Dulmoth Park."

Chapter 17

It was the last day of the holidays. Issie had woken up and felt that strange sense of melancholy that you always get when you know summer is coming to an end. Tomorrow she would be back at school again. Her uniform was already lying on the chair in her bedroom waiting for her. From her bed she could see the blackwatch tartan of her pleated skirt peeking out from beneath the crisp white cotton of her school shirt. Tomorrow she would put her uniform on and begin her fifth-form year at Chevalier Point High School. But today she reached for her jodphurs, pulled on her favourite T-shirt and headed out of the door.

A week had passed since Cassandra Steele had offered

Tom Avery the position of head trainer at Dulmoth Park Stables. Avery had been so shocked at the time, he could barely speak. He just managed to stammer out "I'll think about it". The real surprise came on Monday when Chevalier Point's head instructor phoned Issie up and broke the news that he had accepted!

"I don't believe it!" Issie was stunned. "This is huge!"

"I know," Avery agreed. "I talked it through with Cassandra and I've taken the job – but only with certain conditions attached. I'm more of a cross-country man than a straight showjumper. And it turns out that Cassandra's keen to expand her business and buy some eventing horses. I've taken a good look at Dulmoth Park and I think the farmland has potential. The fields and the forest are perfect terrain – an ideal location for a world-class cross-country course. And with the state-of-the-art stables we can even start our own sporthorse breeding programme."

Cassandra had been won over by Avery's plan to fill the paddocks with future generations of colts and fillies that would grow into great eventing horses. She also agreed when Avery told her that he wanted to hire Verity back as his stable manager.

"Verity knows the routines and requirements of your horses better than anyone," Avery pointed out to Cassandra, "and she's proved that she has the horses' best interests at heart. She was willing to lose her job to keep Tottie healthy. That's the sort of dedication that I'm looking for from my team."

Cassandra Steele didn't need any more convincing. "Get her back immediately and let's get this place humming," she told Tom.

Over the past week, Avery had done exactly that. He had commissioned the world-famous course designer Delaney Swift to work on the new cross-country circuit. Meanwhile, Verity had worked her way through the horses with Avery and between them they had decided who should stay and who should go. Some of Cassandra's showjumpers would be kept, but others would be sold to make way for the young sporthorses. Special stalls would be set up to accommodate the new broodmares and their foals. Avery also contacted all of Ginty's other clients who grazed horses with the stable, the ones that Verity had referred to as the 'weekend rides', and informed them that Ginty had left Dulmoth to set up her own stables and politely suggested that they might like to go with her.

The weekend rides that had been boarding at Dulmoth Park stables would all be moving out over the next two weeks. Only Romeo and Natasha were allowed to stay.

"But you'll have to do your own grooming from now on," Avery told Natasha. "This is a professional stable, and my team has too much work to do to pander to pampered ponies."

Natasha and Issie had both got their old jobs back for the rest of the holidays. Avery asked Stella and Kate if they wouldn't mind working at the stables to help out for the last week, too, while he looked for another new permanent groom to replace Penny. The girls leapt at the chance. "Much more fun than stocking supermarket shelves!" Stella had said gleefully.

Issie gave Stella and Kate a tour of the place on their first day and had loved seeing the looks on her friends' faces as they took in its grandeur.

"This place is, like, totally serious!" Stella had walked into the tack room with her eyes on stalks. "Ohmygod! Is that really an Hermès saddle?"

Verity's arrival back at Dulmoth Park on Monday was greeted with cheers from the other riders. The head groom had left under a cloud but now she was returning as a hero to her new job as stable manager.

"How's Tottie? Can I see her?" Verity asked Avery as soon as she walked through the door.

Tottie hadn't been well at all. The showjumping competition that day had taken its toll on the mare, and when she had returned to Dulmoth Park and the bute finally wore off she was quite lame, barely able to move her hind legs. Avery hadn't held out much hope when he had first examined her. Things looked even more grim when the vet arrived and said that the mare should never have been jumping with such bad arthritis.

"You caught the problem just in time," the vet told them, "If you'd kept on riding her, this mare would have broken down – but arthritis can be managed if you treat it properly and rest the horse."

"Will she ever be sound enough to jump again?" Verity asked anxiously.

"I don't see why not," the vet said, writing something down on his medical pad in illegible scrawl. He handed Verity the prescription. "Keep up this medication, work her in slowly and in another month or so this mare will be better than she ever was."

Verity was so relieved she almost burst into tears. She threw her arms around Tottie's dapple-grey neck, giving the horse a long, hard hug.

When Issie arrived at Dulmoth Park for her last Sunday ride before the holidays were over, the stable grounds looked a bit like a venue for a hunt meet – minus the hounds and the red coats! Along with constructing the new cross-country course it had been Avery's idea to open the grounds up so that members of the Chevalier Point Pony Club could also come and use the facilities at weekends. A steady stream of riders and their horses were already passing through the swanky front gates of the stables.

By the time Issie had saddled up Flame and led him outside to join the others there were at least twenty riders assembled outside the stable block, including Dan and Ben. Dan was riding Madonna and Ben was proudly showing off his new horse, a very handsome sixteen-hand palomino called Shantaram. Ben's surly bay Welsh pony Max had become far too small for him and

Ben had finally faced facts and sold him on. However, his new horse was taking some getting used to.

"He feels really high off the ground," Ben admitted as they milled about in front of the stables waiting for the others to arrive. "I couldn't get my foot in the stirrup to get on him – I had to use a mounting block! If I fall off today I'll never be able to get back on him again!"

Aidan was due to arrive that morning to ride with them, but as ten o'clock loomed and the ride prepared to leave, it looked like he wasn't going to show up. Issic sat on the edge of the group and looked around anxiously for him. This would be their only chance to ride together before he returned to Blackthorn Farm. They had spoken on the phone last night and Aidan had told her he would try to make it. But he still wasn't here and they were about to depart any minute now.

"Are we all ready to go?" Verity called out to the assembled riders.

"Wait for me!" A voice in the distance shouted out, and Issie saw the sliding gates open at the far end of the driveway as Aidan and Fortune came galloping towards the group. Fortune's hooves were churning up the grass verge on the side of the driveway as they galloped and Verity didn't look at all pleased.

"Avery will kill you if you do that again," she told Aidan sharply.

"Sorry, Stable Master!" Aidan said in a cheeky tone. He looked over at Issie and gave her a wink.

"Right!" Verity called out. "Everyone ready? Follow me!"

The ride took them across the acres of farmland at the back of the Dulmoth Park property where Delaney Swift's cross-country course was still in the process of being constructed and down the forest tracks beyond in a long loop around the pond at the southern end of the woods. The whole ride took an hour and a half at a brisk trot, which was a perfect workout for the horses.

The path was narrow and at times the riders had to go single file, but as they got closer to the pond, the track broadened out and they rode side by side.

"So," Aidan said as he pulled up alongside Issie, "I was thinking that you might come back to Blackthorn Farm for the next school holidays…"

Issie nodded. "I've been thinking that too. I haven't seen Aunty Hess in ages and I'd love to come and help out." She smiled. "After all – the three of us are supposed to be business partners, aren't we?"

"I thought I was more than that to you," Aidan said.

Issie smiled at him. "Of course you are," she said softly. "You were my first real boyfriend, Aidan, and you're still one of my best friends – you always will be."

"But," Aidan finished her sentence for her, "you don't want to be my girlfriend any more."

Issie shook her head. "Too much has happened. And we're such good friends. I don't want to ruin that…"

"Hey!" Aidan joked. "It's a bit early in the day to get so deep and meaningful, isn't it?" And then he added quietly in a more sincere tone, "I feel the same way. You're one of my best friends too."

Their special moment was interrupted by Stella cantering up to join them.

"You two looked like you were having a serious discussion so I thought I better come over and get in the way!" she grinned.

"It's OK," Issie laughed. "Serious discussions are over. Let's just enjoy our last day of freedom before we're back at school."

When Issie arrived home that evening she found her mum sorting out white knee socks to go with her brown suede school shoes. "School tomorrow!" Mrs Brown said. "I bet you can't wait!"

"Actually," Issie smiled, "I never thought I'd say this, but I'm looking forward to going back."

She had been thinking a lot lately about last year's report card and her mother's insistence that she take her future seriously. She had put in a special request to make a few changes to her timetable for the new term and now it was jam-packed with swotty subjects like languages and sciences.

Mrs Brown was delighted with her daughter's choices. She might have been slightly less thrilled if she knew the reasons behind them. Issie would need to be able to speak German when she went to Warendorf to train with the best dressage riders in the world. Spanish would come in handy at El Caballo Danza Magnifico. She was even willing to endure Mr Canning's French lessons if it meant she could speak the language fluently when she attended the famous Le Cadre Noir riding school in France. The sciences were essential too. After the dramas with bute and capsaicin in Ginty's illegal medicine chest, Issie figured that every serious horsewoman needed a solid working knowledge of chemistry and biology.

OK, maybe her mum was right and it was a one-in-a-million chance that she would ever have a career as a world-class horse rider. But Issie believed she could do it – and she was going to prove it.

There was only one other crucial detail that had to be resolved if she was really serious about becoming a professional rider. And on Monday, after her first day back at school, she realised that she couldn't put it off any longer. So instead of riding her bike home from school that evening, she cycled along the main road all the way to Dulmoth Park.

At the stables, she parked her bike and grabbed a couple of carrots out of the feed room, then went out to the paddocks behind the arena.

In the field full of horses she spotted Flame immediately. The handsome chestnut was grazing contentedly at the far end of the paddock, but as soon as he heard Issie's voice calling to him he looked up and came trotting to the fenceline to greet her. She felt her heart beat faster as he ran towards her. His paces were so floaty, he looked incredible. It still seemed remarkable to her that such a beautiful, exotic Hanoverian was hers to ride whenever she wanted.

Far from being disappointed with Flame's third place at the North Island show, it turned out Cassandra was extremely pleased with his progress. So much so that she specifically requested that Issie be allowed to continue to work for the stables on a part-time basis once she went back to school so she could ride the stunning chestnut twice a week and take him to the occasional showjumping competition.

"Hey, boy," Issie murmured to Flame. "I've got carrots." And she pulled two bright orange juicy ones out from the pockets of her schoolbag and fed them to the horse, letting him nibble them off the flat of her palm, feeling his whiskers tickling against her skin.

She was looking forward to riding the rest of the season on the big chestnut. They were entered in a one metre jumping class this weekend. Issie had her jodhpurs in her schoolbag and was planning to take Flame for a ride that evening. They would hack out across the fields of Dulmoth Park and down through the forest. But before she could saddle up and ride, she had her future to take care of. She couldn't wait any longer. She had to talk to Avery.

She found Chevalier Point's head instructor sitting behind the desk in his office shuffling his way through a vast stack of paperwork. When Ginty had occupied this office it had a neat, pristine quality about it, but already in just one week Avery had managed to reduce the desk to a messy pile of papers and the floor was littered with bits of grubby horse tack and muddy riding boots.

"I'm thinking of getting an office manager," Avery admitted, as Issie stepped her way around the mess to reach the desk and take seat. "Or at least a cleaner!" he added, looking despairingly at the squalor around him.

"I like it better like this," Issie smiled. "It reminds me of your office at Winterflood Farm."

"Don't even mention that!" Avery groaned. "I'm having trouble juggling my double-life at the moment. Make that triple-life if you count the pony club! I messed up the feeding roster last night and got stuck here until late. By the time I got home to give Starlight, Vinnie and Cookie their hard feeds it was eight o'clock and they weren't pleased! I don't know how I'm going to have time for it all. I'm thinking I'll work from the farm office a couple of days each week and leave Verity in charge here so that I can divide my time…"

Avery realised that he was babbling. "I'm sorry. You don't need to hear the details of my work schedule. How was your first day back at school? It's your fifth-form year, isn't it? Very important. You must have quite a few big decisions to make."

"I do," Issie said. "Well, actually, I have kind of made one. A big decision. That's why I'm here…"

Avery looked at her. "This sounds serious."

Issie nodded. "Tom, I keep thinking about what happened. You warned me right from the start about working for Ginty, and I should have believed you—"

"Issie," Avery cut her off, "I told you. We don't need to talk about this again. You've apologised and I completely understand. Sometimes we need to find these things out for ourselves. You couldn't have known what Ginty was really like."

"But I should have realised sooner!" Issie said. "The moment I saw her rapping the horses I knew deep down inside that it was wrong. She was just so convincing, Tom. And part of me wanted to believe her. I wanted to prove that I could handle myself and I didn't need your help any more."

Issie looked down at her feet, hesitating, scared to speak. "But I realise now that I need your help more than ever. If I'm serious about really wanting a career as an international eventing rider, then I can't do it by myself."

She smiled hopefully at him. "Tom, I need you to be my instructor."

"But Issie," Avery looked puzzled, "I am your instructor."

"I know," Issie said. "I mean I need you to coach me like a professional. I know you're busy. And I know it will cost me money and I'm totally going to pay you—"

"Issie." Avery held up his hand to stop her. "Do you mean it? Are you serious about this? A career as an international eventing rider is going to be hard work. It's going to take up every last scrap of your time and commitment. Your world will become nothing but horses. You'll have to fit in your schoolwork of course, that's a given, but apart from that you won't have time for anything else. We're talking about a gruelling physical training schedule here, and it's risky too. Eventing is the most dangerous sport in the world bar none. I know you have the talent – but a true professional rider also needs drive, commitment and absolute unwavering dedication. Are you really and truly ready for this?"

"I am. Tom, I want to be an international eventing rider and I'll do anything it takes to make it."

"OK, then," Avery said.

"OK?" Issie frowned. "That's it? I tell you I want to be a world-class rider and you just say 'OK'?"

"Uh-huh." Avery began to hunt around distractedly, pushing aside the piles of papers on his desk.

"Aha! Here it is!" he announced victoriously as he pulled out a little black address book. Now he began to thumb through the pages, muttering to himself as he went through the alphabetical listings.

"Ummmm, Tom?" Issie said. "What are you doing?"

"You want to be a world-class eventing rider, right?"

Avery said. "I think you've made your case pretty clear."

"Uh-huh," Issie said. "So now what? What are you up to?"

"I'm making a phone call," Avery told her. "The first step to becoming a champion eventing rider is to get you the right horse. We need a true athlete with the ability to go all the way."

"I've been thinking about that," Issie said. "I thought maybe Cassandra Steele could sponsor me and—"

"Yes, yes, that's an excellent idea," Avery said, "Cassandra might like to sponsor you at some stage. But she doesn't have to buy you a world-class eventing horse, Issie. You've already got one."

"What are you talking about?" Issie said. "And who are you phoning?"

Avery picked up the receiver. "I'm calling Francoise."

And suddenly Issie knew exactly where this was heading. By the time she left Avery's office half an hour later, plans were already underway. Very soon they would be going to Spain, where they would see old friends and collect on a promise that had been made long ago. If Avery was right, then the Spanish trip would be just the beginning of an even greater journey – into the world of international eventing. They would bring back the horse that would help Issie to realise her dreams and compete against the best riders in the world.

Issie had been waiting for this moment for so long, she couldn't believe it was here at last. Her colt was going to be returned to her.

Nightstorm was coming home to Chevalier Point.

STACY GREGG

PONY  CLUB SECRETS

Angel and the Flying stallions

Issie's colt, Storm, has finally finished his training and he's ready to be reunited with her in Spain! To get him back, Issie must prove herself by riding the complex moves of haute école on stallion Angel. Meanwhile, there's a mystery at El Caballo stables as their best mares begin to disappear . . .

HarperCollins *Children's Books*

STACY GREGG

PONY CLUB SECRETS

Book One

Mystic and the Midnight Ride

Issie LOVES horses and is a member of the Chevalier Point Pony Club, where she looks after her pony Mystic, trains for gymkhanas and hangs out with her best friends.

When Issie is asked to train Blaze, an abandoned pony, her riding skills are put to the test. Can she tame the spirited new horse? And is Blaze really out of danger?

HarperCollins *Children's Books*

STACY GREGG

PONY  CLUB SECRETS

Book Two

Blaze and the Dark Rider

Issie and her friends have been picked to represent the
Chevalier Point Pony Club at the Interclub Shield – the
biggest competition of the year. It's time to get training!

But when equipment is sabotaged and one of the riders
is injured, Issie and her friends are determined to find
out who's to blame...

HarperCollins *Children's Books*

STACY GREGG

PONY CLUB SECRETS

Book Three

Destiny and the Wild Horses

Issie goes mad when she finds out she'll be staying with her aunt for the summer. What about the dressage competition she and Blaze have been training so hard for, and her friends at the Chevalier Point Pony Club?

When she finds out Blaze can go with her, and she'll be helping to train movie-star horses, Issie's summer starts to look a whole lot more interesting...

HarperCollins *Children's Books*

STACY GREGG

PONY  CLUB SECRETS

Book Four

Stardust and the Daredevil Ponies

Issie has landed her dream job – handling horses on a real film set! And with a group of frisky palominos to deal with, Issie's pony-club friends get to help out too.

What is spoilt star Angelique's big secret? Could this be Issie's chance for stardom?

HarperCollins *Children's Books*

STACY GREGG

PONY  CLUB SECRETS

Book Five

Comet and the Champion's Cup

Issie's aunt needs experts to help run her summer riding school. The perfect way for Issie and her friends to spend the holidays! Issie forms a special bond with Comet, a feisty pony with the talent to jump like a superstar. But can she train him in time for the Horse of the Year Show?

HarperCollins *Children's Books*